THE FIFTH SEAL

By Paul Nilsen

AmErica House
Baltimore

First printing

ISBN: 1-59129-162-3
PUBLISHED BY AMERICA HOUSE BOOK PUBLISHERS
www.publishamerica.com
Baltimore

Printed in the United States of America

~ Dedication ~

The writing of this book came as a surprise to me. Firstly, I need to thank my daughter Abigail. I began this project as a joke, in order to encourage you to use and develop your own writing skills. As you promised, now that it is published, you have to read it. Secondly, I need to thank my son Josiah. You were my greatest fan. Your daily interest in whether I had written anything new let me know that the book was interesting, at least to you. Thirdly, I need to thank my wife. You are my most honest critic. When you think I have a bad idea, you let me know about it. In a similar way, when I have a good idea or do something well you encourage me in it. Your encouragement about the early chapters of the book, helped to keep me writing. Whether you think my ideas bad or good, you are always supportive. Thank you Sherri. I love you. My other children played important roles as well. Joel, your constant wanting to play on the computer helped me to write fast. Hannah and Jonathan, thanks for letting me know when I needed a break, and that there were more important things in life than writing a book. We had fun laughing about dad writing a book and what its title would be.

Jan, thank you for your help and suggestions on grammar and writing style. I incorporated almost all the changes you suggested and the book is better because of it.

Thank you, America House, for your willingness to publish new authors, and for all your work in making this book a reality.

Thank you, reader, for being interested enough to read this book. I hope you enjoy it and in some way are benefitted by it.

~Sincerely, Paul Nilsen

I dedicate this book, to the greater glory of God, my Creator, my Redeemer, my Father, and my Friend.

Chapter 1

Pastor Jim Allen stood overlooking his adopted town of Green Bluff, Wisconsin. His mind was full of questions and doubts, his heart full of fear. It had been two months earlier that he had sent away his wife, Sandy, and his children, Caleb, Ashley, and Carol, to live with his in-laws. Now it was his turn to flee from their home. In spite of the warm weather, his body was trembling. Fifteen minutes earlier he had received a call from his friend, Tom Watson, a town councilman from Green Bluff. The call had been brief and to the point. Tom had been emphatic. Jim had to flee from his house immediately if he hoped to escape with his freedom and perhaps with his life. Though unwanted, the call had not been unexpected. Jim asked Tom only one question, "Are they coming for me only or for the whole church?"

Jim had to act quickly, but he had been prepared for some time now.

After hanging up the phone, Jim called Sven Svensen, one of the elders of Green Bluff Baptist Church who had remained faithful to Christ and who had been unwavering in his support of Jim's pastoral leadership of the church. Tom had assured Jim that for now, the arrest order carried only one name: Jim's. Sven and the other church members would be safe for the time being, but they would have to act with greater caution. As they had discussed and agreed upon earlier, the church would no longer meet in the church building but in alternating houses, barns, and country areas. Jim would make contact with them as he could. His first priority now, though, was his family.

Following the phone call to elder Svensen, Jim left and locked the house. He taped a note on the front door. It read, "Dear Ron, Sorry, I had to go out because of an urgent call. I don't know how long I will be gone. My mobile phone is broken. Please call me at home or stop by around 10:00 p.m. tonight." Jim had no intention of being home at that time, but he hoped that the note would delay his pursuers long enough for him to make a successful escape. Though meant to deceive, Jim calmed his conscience with the fact that the literal content of the message was accurate. His clothes had already been packed and placed in the trunk of his car a month earlier, along with their family tent, a few sleeping bags, and some emergency supplies. Jim had closed out his bank account three weeks previous, and he carried with him the money that he had not already left with his wife on his visit to see her two weeks earlier. In case anyone had seen him leaving town, he first drove south, and then, cutting back through some dirt farming roads, made his way west to Swede's Hill.

Swede's Hill was the bluff from which Green Bluff appropriately got it's name. Though far from being a mountain, the broad, densely wooded top of Swede's Hill was the highest elevation in the area. The hill itself was named after a Swedish hermit who lived there in the early days when the area was first settled.

Jim normally would have reveled in the spectacular beauty of the fall colors. Before his eyes, an array of orange, red, yellow, and green leaves contrasted with the deep brown of newly plowed fields and the dark blue of the late afternoon sky. Fall was Jim's favorite season, and no one could have asked for a finer fall day. Caught up, however, in his own thoughts, Jim scarcely noticed his surroundings. Driving up Swede's Hill, his only thought regarding the season was gladness that much of the foliage was still on the trees. Were it a month later, it would be much more difficult to hide, should hiding be necessary. It was Tuesday, October 15, a year from the date of the fateful announcements made in Prague.

Jim pulled his car off of the road near the lake, into an area shaded by large maple trees and thick with undergrowth of blackberry bushes and saplings. Before moving to the stand of trees from which he could see the town and the road leading up to Swede's Hill, Jim took the precaution of chopping down some of the saplings to cover over his vehicle. He felt as if he were playing a role in a television adventure/thriller. It was a new feeling, and one he didn't like. While Jim led an active life and had never shied away from controversy, he had never courted danger for danger's sake.

Jim Allen was to some degree a product of the church. His parents, now dead, had taken Jim to church from the time he was four years old. His father, a former steel worker from Pittsburgh, Pennsylvania, had accepted Christ as a result of the persistent testimony of a co-worker. Eager to share his new found joy with his family, the following Sunday found the Allen family in the pews of Faith Baptist Church. There, through the loving attention of the members of the church and the clear biblical teaching of the pastor, Jim's mother soon surrendered her life to Christ as Savior and Lord. Along with school and sports and family vacations, much of Jim's earlier life was spent in the context of the activities of Faith Baptist Church. Worship services, sunday school, vacation bible school, youth meetings and Christian camp were as normal a part of his life as eating and sleeping. And to tell the truth, Jim had enjoyed his upbringing and had eagerly absorbed and participated in the faith of those who surrounded him. He was somewhat surprised in his elementary school years when he realized that everybody did not live more or less the way he and his family did. He remembered how it had angered him when his friend, Frank, had to move away because his parents had gotten divorced. How could they do that, he had wondered. Jesus didn't want that. But Frank and his family didn't know Jesus and had only been in a church a few times in their lives. In his innocence, Jim had wondered why somebody would decide not to go to church and why they would choose to live in a way that brought them pain instead of obeying Jesus.

As he passed though his teen years, Jim continued in his innocence to the ways of evil, though he became increasingly aware of the many who willfully became its prey. He faced the temptations of his youth and the questions of a doubting society in the context of his faith in Jesus. He could not remember an exact date or experience of conversion, but he knew upon whom he believed. It was with the joy and support of his family that Jim decided at the age of 14 to give public confession of his faith in Christ by asking to be baptized. It was later with similar joy that his parents listened to Jim as he expressed his desire to go to Bible school to prepare to be a pastor. His mother died before he was ordained to the Christian ministry in the first church over which he pastored, but he felt he could always feel the hands of his father laid upon him that day, as his father joined with others to pray over him, asking the Lord's blessing on his life and ministry.

How he longed now for his father's presence and counsel as he stood looking down on the town from which he fled. Dad would know what to say or do even in these difficult circumstances.

Jim had met his wife, Sandy, on one of the evangelistic outreaches in which he had participated while in Bible School. The singing group of which he was a part did a tour of the northern midwestern states, ministering largely in smaller country churches that had had some connection to Bible College where he attended. Sandy was the daughter of a Wisconsin dairy farmer, John Peterson, who happened to offer his home as sleeping quarters for two of the young men from the group. Mr. Peterson always denied any intentions of matchmaking, saying it had only been an act of Christian hospitality. In fact, his daughter never needed help in the area of securing dates. Her slim figure and her Nordic features, coupled with an easy going personality and a ready smile, kept a steady stream of hopefuls at the door.

It was a brief meeting, but one in which an interest was sparked on both parts. Jim, having no trouble with his eyesight, was attracted by Sandy's beauty. Sandy was drawn to Jim by the sincerity of his commitment to Christ, an area in which many of her other would be suitors were sorely lacking. Through letters and visits this spark was fanned into a flame, and the year following Jim's graduation from Bible School the two were married. Following the death of Jim's dad in 2007, Jim and Sandy decided to look for a church closer to Sandy's family. In January of the following year, they said their good-byes to the church they were serving in Cleveland, Ohio, and with their 3-year-old son Caleb, set off with great anticipation to their new post in Green Bluff.

The early years of their ministry at Green Bluff Baptist Church were happy ones. As with any transition of pastoral leadership, there were adjustments to be made both on Jim and Sandy's part, as well as on the part of the congregation, but from the start it had been a good match-up. Sandy helped Jim a great deal in adjusting from his city background to the rural setting of Green Bluff. Things were more tranquil in the country. His ministry needed to focus more on people than on programs and promotion. Participation in community affairs took on a priority that it had not had in his previous pastorate in Cleveland. It was through his involvement with Little League baseball that his friendship with Tom Watson began. Church growth and fiery preaching took a back seat to authentic Christian living and ministering to the real and felt needs of his congregation and community. Many times this meant sitting for an hour with an older person as he recounted tales of his past, or helping a neighbor chop and load wood that they would need for warmth during the winter months. Jim had adjusted quickly to these changes and appreciated the slower pace of life. In Green Bluff, he was allowed and even encouraged to make family time a priority. Ashley and Carol soon joined brother Caleb. The Allen family was truly happy.

Green Bluff Baptist Church was also happy with its new pastor. The church was incorporated in the year 1864 as a Swedish speaking Free Church. As families from other nationalities moved into the area, and as the sons and daughters of the original Swedish immigrants began to adapt more and more to the English language and American culture, the church saw its need to change. From 1869 through 1878, there were some church services held in English and others in Swedish. In 1878, it was voted that all services and outreaches of the church would be held in English. Though the majority of the members continued to be of Swedish heritage, the name of the church was officially changed from the Swedish Free Church of Green Bluff to the name that it currently held, Green Bluff Baptist Church. Its church building had been in the center of town, but as the town and church grew it was seen necessary to move the church facilities to a new and more expansive location. In 1957 after much discussion, the original church building was sold (it now being a craft shop) and ground was bought on the western outskirts of the town. A church sanctuary, educational wing, and parsonage had since been built, providing very adequate facilities for the 120 member congregation.

When Jim and Sandy arrived and began their ministry, the church had been averaging an attendance of approximately 90 people in the Sunday service. The previous pastor, Pastor Edgar, was an older man who had retired and moved to live nearer his children and grandchildren in the southwestern part of the state. He continued to be active in ministry, preaching in his area as requested. He had been a much beloved pastor in Green Bluff and visited there a couple of times each year. He was supportive of Jim's ministry, and Jim considered him a valued counselor. Pastor Edgar had, however, in the final years of his ministry in Green Bluff, lost much of his steam and energy. Health problems of one nature or another often limited his being able to visit the congregation or to personally reach out to new families. The church had been more or less in a holding pattern during those years with much of the effort of the congregation being focused inwardly toward ministering to themselves. As Jim adjusted to the town and rural ministry, the church began to grow. It was not a drastic or sudden growth, but new life was being breathed into the congregation. Seeing new faces in the services of the church encouraged the long-standing members. What a joy it was to see these lives which had been changed by their newly owned faith in Christ!

Life was good. Jim often thought about how blessed he was to be a Christian. He loved to consider passages such as Joshua 1:8,9, Psalm 1, and Psalm 23, which speak of the prosperity of the Christian and how everything will turn out well for those who meditate on and put into practice God's Word. He could sing out with David in Psalms 3:8, that God's blessing indeed rested upon His people. He could testify, as David did in Psalms 16:6, that the boundary lines of his life had fallen for him in pleasant places and that he enjoyed a delightful inheritance from his heavenly Father. He loved God. He loved his congregation and community. He loved his wife and family. And he felt loved in return. For many of these early years in Green Bluff Jim's life was reflected in the words made famous by the beer advertisements from his teen years: "It doesn't get any better than this." Jim could remember seeing those commercials during the breaks of Monday Night Football. "Those guys didn't have a clue," Jim thought. Life was good, but Jim knew that it was going to get better, much better, soon. What he was living then was nothing compared to what life was going to be like when Jesus came back for him in the clouds to take him to his heavenly home. Oh how he longed for that day.

What he did not know in those years and what had caught him so much by surprise, was, that before that glorious moment of being raptured up into the heavens to be with Jesus, his idyllic life would disappear before his eyes. Standing on the bluffs which overlooked the town which had become his home and considering the words of his friend, Tom Watson, he doubted now whether the rapture would ever occur. He was tired. He had been abandoned and ridiculed by those he had called brothers. His faith had undergone more trials than he could now recount and was at a breaking point.

Chapter 2

Tom's call was the culmination of a long series of events which Jim had initially greeted with great enthusiasm.

The town council, with pressure from the state and national government, had been dropping hints, some of them none too subtle, regarding the offensive messages that Jim had been preaching from the pulpit of the small Baptist Church which he pastored in Green Bluff. Laws had recently been enacted in the United States Congress which prohibited sectarianism and the spread of intolerance. To proclaim that the Bible was God's Word and that salvation was by faith in Jesus Christ alone, a freedom which had been enjoyed in the United States since its founding as a nation, was now considered factious, dangerous to the well-being of society and its citizens, and as of three months earlier, illegal. The declaration of freely chosen lifestyles to be immoral and sinful, was now determined to be hatred, bigotry, and slander, and became punishable by law.

Jim, to his credit, although aware of the laws, felt bound by his convictions and his love for Christ. As long as he was able, he had determined that he would be faithful to preach what he believed with all his heart and mind to be the literal Word of God.

It was because of what the Bible said that the events of the previous years had at first so excited Jim. He saw the prophesies of the Bible concerning the end times being fulfilled right before his eyes. He felt sure that Christ would soon return for his church, judge the world, and establish his millennial reign. Everything that he had read in the papers seemed to confirm this belief. First, there had been the peaceful conquering, or coming together, of the European nations. What no dictator nor emperor had been able to accomplish in war had been accomplished in diplomacy. What seemed to have been a far off dream for many, when Jim was a little boy, had become a reality. It made all earthly sense that the nations should have joined. The Euro and the European common passport facilitated commerce and travel between the nations. The joining together of the stock markets of the individual countries had, in time, converted the European Union into the strongest economic block in the world. The uniting of their military forces into the European United Defense Force for the Advancement of World Peace had several years earlier replaced the antiquated (from the European point of view) North Atlantic Treaty Organization, which the Europeans had always felt was unfairly dominated by the United States. Its mission, as its name indicated, went well beyond defensive purposes to the promotion of European values throughout the globe. The Union itself, beginning rather humbly with the participation of six Western European nations, had subsequently grown to gigantic proportions. It grew to include the Eastern European nations, with an associate membership extended to the British Commonwealth and the Portuguese speaking South American nations. The countries that did not form a direct part of the European Union were being influenced greatly by it, many of them hoping to be admitted into it as a member nation. The formation of the European Union had not been without its problems and pitfalls, but Jim had no doubt that it was the one world government prophesied in Revelation chapter 13 and Daniel 7.

Second, Jim had witnessed in his lifetime an amazing coming together of the world's religions under the authority of Rome. The Roman Catholic Church, beginning with Vatican 2, had undertaken an aggressive ecumenical campaign. This campaign became personified in the person of Pope John Paul II. Jim remembered clearly the year 2000, proclaimed by the Pope to be a year of jubilee. In it, though failing in health, Pope John Paul II reached out in every direction. Agreements and joint confessions of faith were made by the Catholic Church with such diverse groups as the Anglicans, the Lutherans, the Orthodox Churches, the Muslims, the Jews, the Hindus, and with many noted evangelical leaders. The Pope's picture was almost constantly in the news holding hands with or embracing the leaders of these other faiths. The call was continually being extended for peace and religious unity, not on the basis of doctrine, but on the basis of leadership; the leadership of the Vatican. In the years following 2000, because of the advancement of the Parkinson's Disease from which he suffered, John Paul II was unable to travel as often as he had done previously. The bridges, however, had been established and the religious leaders of the world went to him at the Vatican, seeking his advice and counsel and forming ever stronger ties with Rome. One of his great legacies, though the actual rebuilding occurred several years after his death, was the agreement between the Jews and the Muslims, brokered by the Catholic Church, which allowed for the rebuilding of the Jewish Temple and the reestablishment of their religious sacrifices on the Temple Mount next to the Muslim shrine of the Dome of the Rock. When Jim was a teenager, such an agreement would have been impossible and acceptable neither to the Jews nor the Muslims, but unimaginable and incredible changes had taken place.

Pope John Paul II was almost impossible not to like. His quiet charismatic personality, his kissing of the ground of each country he visited, his intelligence and strength of moral leadership, and his perseverance and uncomplaining attitude in the face of illness made him legendary. Perhaps for this reason, news of his death was greeted by worldwide grief. As so often happens when a great leader dies, both those inside and outside the Church of Rome were asking themselves, "What will we do now? How can we ever replace Pope John Paul?"

As the selection of Karol Wojtyla to be the leader of the Roman Catholic Church was somewhat of a surprise in October of 1978, of equal surprise was the selection of his successor, a cardinal who assumed the name Pope Adrian VII. His selection had been a coup of sorts for the Jesuit order, which had been criticized by Pope John Paul II for the emphasis that many of its priests placed on social and political involvement, many times in opposition to the official teachings of the Roman Church. The very selection of the name Adrian VII signaled the new Pope's intentions to liberalize and politicize the church over which he had been given charge. Pope Adrian I had been one of the most politically active popes in the history of the church, and was responsible for the initial formation of the Papal States. Adrian VII followed in his footsteps. As John Paul II had worked hard to develop a unity of religions under the Roman Church, Adrian VII, in his earlier years as Pope, cultivated his relationship with the political leaders of the world, especially the leaders of the European Union. At times it had been difficult to distinguish between the affirmations of this great political body and those of the Roman Church. If there did not exist a cause and effect relationship between the two bodies, political and religious, it seemed obvious that there was an ever growing cooperation between the two.

A second emphasis change in the Roman Church, under the authority of Adrian VII, had been in the social and moral realm. If there was one large group which had felt ostracized by the leadership of Pope John Paul II, it was, to put a name to them, the seculars within the church and society, who criticized the church's stand against abortion, birth control, homosexuality, and women in the priesthood. John Paul II had been unmoving in these areas and had sought to promote to the office of Cardinal those who agreed with his conservative moral stance. Pope Adrian VII, however, was determined to reach out to this group and was willing to change the church's position on these issues to be able to do so. Of course, this was the change many had been hoping and calling for for many years. Thousands came streaming into the church which had essentially been remade to accommodate them. The church, instead of being criticized as it had been over the centuries for its stand on moral absolutes, now joined its voice with those who had criticized it. What was sinful now, according to the Roman Catholic Church, were not actions which violated the commands of God, but rather a critical or judgmental attitude towards another because of the way in which he or she had freely chosen to live.

One would think that such a drastic reversal concerning so many of its core moral and spiritual issues would have caused a major conflict and split within the church. It is true that there were those who left the church because of this reason, but they were few. Jim thought of the two families that had left the Roman Catholic Church in anger and disillusionment over their church's approval of homosexual relationships and abortion, and who had since joined Green Bluff Baptist Church. But why hadn't there been more of an upheaval among the morally conservative members of the Roman Church? Part of it, of course, had to do with the acceptance on the part of the people (especially among the practicing Catholics) of the authority of the Pope and the cardinals. Did not God act through them infallibly? Were not they, as laity, to trust in the established leadership? But there had been another, stronger factor. Where Pope

Adrian VII went, miracles occurred. At first they were few and directly related to the needs of the people. There were people who had been blind who now could see. There were people who had been deaf who now heard. Individuals who had incurable diseases were declared healed by the testimony of many physicians. Such miracles increased, so much so that, at the hands of Pope Adrian, the people came to the point where they not only hoped to be healed, but expected it. In time, there were other signs as well. Signs of power and authority. As he had healed, so he also began to curse some who opposed him. Great multitudes followed him in awe. Others were devoted to him out of love for what he had done for them or for a loved one. Still others yielded to his authority in fear. Many saw in these miracles the hand and blessing of God. Jim recognized a different power at work. Could this have been anyone other than the second beast mentioned in Revelation 13?

Jim had considered these events with mounting excitement and enthusiasm. He had preached repeatedly to his congregation that the Lord's return was at hand and that He would rapture His church from the earth before the great tribulation and suffering to come. He had not set any dates or hours for this event for which he so longed, but he had been sure that it was imminent. He had stopped preaching regarding spiritual growth issues in the church and had focused almost exclusively on evangelism and the need for people to accept Christ's salvation that very day. Those who trusted Christ would not suffer. Those who refused to trust in Him would suffer as no one had since the beginning of the world. Despite the difficult situation in which he now found himself, or perhaps because of it, the remembrance of such messages caused within him an ironic laugh. How zealous he had been and his zeal had to some degree become infectious. Several within the congregation had begun to witness to their friends and neighbors as they never had before. Parroting some of Jim's messages, they pointed people to the events of the day, showing them the Scriptures regarding the end times and emphasizing the blessed hope of the rapture. Many new people were added to the ranks of the church, eager to escape the wrath to come.

But then things began to go wrong.

Chapter 3

As the events began to change so did Jim's perspective of them. He began to feel as if he were in a room which had no exit where the walls were slowly drawing in, closer and closer. He tried to deny what was happening. His beliefs on what would occur in the end times did not permit him to conceive of a world-wide suffering of Christ's church to the degree that it was now occurring, and which had now become very personal. Even as he had listened to Tom's voice on the telephone, he wanted to think that it was all a bad joke or a nightmare from which he would wake up. He wanted to argue with Tom, that what Tom was saying could not be true. But Jim knew that it was true. He could feel, as it were, the cold concrete of the walls beginning to press against his flesh, crushing him.

Of course, it was true that throughout the history of the church men and women had suffered and died for their faith in Jesus Christ. Jim had often been challenged by reading of the early martyrs of the church: Steven, James, the disciples, Justin Martyr, Polycarp. "The blood of the martyrs is the seed of the church," was a quote he had heard and repeated many times. Surely, as the gospel advanced into godless cultures and peoples it would be met with resistance. Casualties, though unfortunate, were to be expected. Satan was not to be expected to give up his ground easily, but the promise of Christ that the gates of hell would not prevail against the establishment of his church had been proven again and again. In time, with persistent witness, often costing the lives of the earlier heralds, the church of Jesus had been established throughout all parts of the world.

Jim also knew that the twentieth century, in which he had passed the earlier years of his life, saw the martyrdom of more Christians than the previous 19 centuries combined. But was it not also the century in which Christ's church had advanced into more unreached people groups with the gospel than any other previous century? Tribes that nobody ever knew existed before had been found by

Christian missionaries. Green Bluff Baptist Church had played its part it this effort, praying for and financially helping to support many missionaries to other lands. As the battle fronts increased, was it not logical that the body count would increase as well? As real Christianity attempted to advance into Communist and Muslim strongholds, was it not to be expected that there would be suffering on the part of the early believers in these areas? Jim had considered the high rate of Christian martyrs in the 20th century one of the signs of triumph and advancement toward the completion of the Great Commission to which Jesus had called his followers. And as some died, many more believed and the church grew and became established. Indeed, it was declared by missions experts that the Great Commission, which Christ had given to His disciples in Matthew 28:18-20, had been fulfilled. While there were still many who did not know Christ, there were now at least some individuals of every identifiable ethnic group who proclaimed Him as Lord and Savior.

Jim had felt that he himself had been willing to so risk his life in a foreign part of the world in order that people there should hear of Jesus and believe upon Him. The quote of Jim Elliot, martyr at the hands of the Auca Indians in Ecuador, "He is no fool who loses that which he cannot keep to gain that which he cannot lose," had inspired Jim as a teen and taught him that true life was to be found in abandoning it in service to Christ.

But a very different type of martyrdom had begun to spring up. It was one which Jim had not expected. It was the advancement of Satan against the church. The martyrdom had in fact begun many years earlier with the assassination of the Christian mind-set. The observations made by Charles Darwin in the mid-1800's about the evolution of biological life within species were blown all out of proportion by him and others, to suggest that all life is the product of pure happenstance. From some unknown and non-intelligent eternal matter (probably a gas), had evolved the universe and all the variety and complexity of earthly plant, animal, and human life. Those that wished to deny the existence of an intelligent, all-powerful creator proclaimed their message long enough and loudly enough that somehow it became the accepted theory of the origin of life, and consequently the governing philosophy regarding all aspects of human thought and society. "God is dead," proclaimed many, not to say that He had existed and then died, but rather to say that He had never really existed in the first place. He was a crutch that primitive man had created and upon which he could lean and trust. Such mythology was not necessary for the evolved modern man.

The Bible, according to this philosophy, was not the revelation of God to man. Rather it was the product of man's evolving religious and philosophical thought. It was not a book to be believed and followed. Rather it only served as a curious study regarding the simple minded beliefs of our less advanced ancestors. Surely there were some lofty thoughts and concepts contained therein that still maintained a value for the present day, but modern man in his increased knowledge was to be the judge of such matters.

The philosophy of evolution invaded all levels of society and reached into every institution, including theologically conservative Christian universities and seminaries. Pastors began to discard the use of the Bible and deny the supernatural intervention of God in the affairs of the world and mankind. Jim had been keenly aware from the time of his later high school years that his beliefs placed him in a small minority. His belief in the Bible (the whole Bible) as the literal Word of God and his faith in Jesus as Savior and Lord made him an intellectual and social oddball. But at the time, it did not make him an outcast. If there were times that Jim did not participate with his peers, it was because of his own decision to opt out of activities which he knew were displeasing to God. His friends would often joke with him about his refusal to "party" with them, with all that entailed, but they gave him room to be himself and even respected him for his consistency and integrity of life. Jim was a necessary part of stimulating conversations, because he was one of the few who presented an opposing view to the unified thinking of the others. Of course there were always a few belligerent crusaders who would take it upon themselves to ridicule his beliefs and to attack them at every opportunity. Jim had felt especially sorry for them and wondered what inner hurts and needs drove them to such antagonism.

In Green Bluff there were seven churches. Of the seven, only two, Green Bluff Baptist Church and Lutheran Evangelical Trinity Church, held to a high view of Bible inspiration and authority. The

21

others, especially in recent years, openly declared it to be man's word about God, much of which was obviously erroneous. Jim, when he first arrived in Green Bluff, had attended the meetings of the clergy fellowship of the town. He had ceased going some four years earlier, however, as a result of irreconcilable differences. Jim simply could not consent to many of the declarations put forth by the fellowship, nor could he participate gladly in the activities that were suggested for their times of joint worship. For their part, the other ministers had tired long since of Jim's statement, "But the Bible says..." He was not missed at the meetings.

Satan directed his second wave of attack against Christian morals. Though the United States was not and never had been a Christian nation, according to Jim's point of view, it had respected, encouraged, and even enforced Christian moral values throughout most of its history. It was called the Judeo-Christian heritage, and found its expression in the Ten Commandments and the teachings of Jesus and the apostles. There had always been those who had chosen to live outside those values, but they had been the minority and had to endure family and societal disapproval for their sinful ways. Homosexuality took place in the closet. Pornography had to be sought out in the dark streets of the inner city, and those who went in search of it often went disguised to hide their shame. Abortion procedures took place in back alleys. Drunks carried their bottles in paper bags. Young couples who decided to be sexually active had to search for a place where it would be neither seen nor known. Divorce was difficult to obtain and often only in proven cases of infidelity and abuse, where the guilty spouse would have no rights following the divorce. More than a few couples were surprised by joy as they had to make the hard adjustments necessary to make their marriage work. Cursing was corrected, not broadcast. Thieves and murderers actually went to jail.

The popular belief that God either did not exist, or if He did exist, was unknowable, led to the logical conclusion that absolute moral law did not exist. If God did not exist, who was to say what was right or wrong? Did right and wrong even exist? The idea of sin became archaic. No one had the right to say that what another person was doing was wicked.

While the foundations for the attack on Christian morals were laid with the advance of evolutionary thinking, the fruits thereof began to show themselves in the late 1950's and early 1960's. The family was the first to come under fire, as divorce rates began to rise. In the late sixties and early seventies the hippie movement exploded, with its glorification of "sex, drugs, and rock'n roll." What began as a rebellion soon became mainstream, protected and promoted by governmental laws and money. What is more, it became increasingly mainstream within the church. On the one hand, there were those churches that put up no resistance to the changes and even embraced them in their "worship." Jim remembered with disgust the last united "worship" service of the clergy fellowship of Green Bluff that he had attended. In a liturgical dance entitled, "Naked Before God," the central character, "God," was progressively stripping away the cloths of the other dancers, entitled, "fear," "inhibitions," "self doubt," etc... Jim began to get nervous, as fewer and fewer clothes remained. When the breasts were bared, Jim made for the exit, glad that he had some time earlier ceased to make mention of these meetings to his congregation. He never went back to another one of the clergy fellowship meetings.

On the other hand, those churches which still held to the Bible as God's Word were increasingly confronted by difficult situations of moral failure. The instances of unwed pregnancies, abortions, divorce, substance abuse, dishonesty, etc... within the churches, rivaled the statistics of society in general. It was not just people coming new into the church, bringing past problems with them. It was also those who had attended for many years and who had made professions of faith in Christ, including many pastors whom Jim had known. Jim and his board of elders had struggled more often than they had desired to with questions of exhortation, discipline, and restoration, and they knew that they were only touching the tip of the matter and dealing only with the most obvious of the problems. For whatever reason, there were many who wanted to think of themselves as Christians while living their lives as they pleased. There were others who sincerely seemed to want to walk with the Lord, but who seemed unable to stand firm before the multitude of temptations placed before them.

One thing had become clear. To live a Christ-centered, obedient life was, as it had been in the first centuries, counter-cultural. The vast majority followed the playboy philosophy: "If it feels good, do it." Those, like Jim, who attempted to live according to the precept of Jesus, "Lord, not my will, but Thine be done," though numerous, were in the clear minority, even within the church. It had been that way throughout Jim's lifetime. He was used to it. In his prideful moments, he even reveled in his image as a rebel for Christ. Though viewed as odd and often ridiculed and mocked (Christians made great sport for stand up comedians), Christians enjoyed the freedom to live their lives as they felt God wanted and the freedom to proclaim to others their message of a different and better life. That was until the third wave of Satan's attack.

The third wave was the full frontal assault, and it was this that had caught Jim by surprise. Having attacked the Christian way of thinking and the Christian way of life, Satan was going for the knock out punch. The assault began in the countries of the European Union, where the Christian church was small and without worldly influence. Backed by the moral enthusiasm of the Vatican led ecumenical behemoth, laws were passed and put into effect against the public denunciation of lifestyle decisions or moral choices. Public denunciation included printed material and public discourse, including sermons or teachings to one's own church body. Rapidly these laws were broadened to include counseling situations and the instruction of parents to their own children. As the Bible fomented division and prejudice, against witchcraft, homosexuality, adultery, drunkenness, etc..., its printing and public sale or distribution was made illegal and punishable by fines and/or prison sentences for repeated offenses. Bibles already in print were not confiscated, but the Union warned that prejudicial passages were not to be read or taught from. Churches and Bible study groups were infiltrated by new visitors with pens and notebooks in hand, and many were the pastors and lay people who were called to appear before the justice system and first warned and then punished for their divisive spirit. Children in the public schools were given questionnaires about the things that their parents had taught them. If confirmed that the parents had declared to their children that certain actions and/or lifestyles were wrong or sinful, those children were removed from their homes, and boarded and trained in state residential schools. There was little recourse against these actions of the state, other than to renounce one's beliefs before the tribunal.

Jim had been incredulous when he had first heard of these laws, believing them to be the exaggeration of well intentioned but misinformed brethren. As the truth of this persecution was confirmed by many sources, Jim's disbelief turned into concern, prayer, and action. He had personally contacted the offices of his state's senators and the office of his area's representative to the House of Representatives in Washington, DC. He protested what was taking place in the European Union countries and asked that pressure be put on by the United States in order that these laws be changed. He signed and encouraged his congregation to sign a petition to the United Nations, pleading for religious freedom and freedom of expression to be reestablished in Europe. But the truth was, the United States, so long the great power of the world, now held little influence over the affairs of other nations in comparison to its European neighbor. The United Nations was virtually controlled by the European Union, for the European Union, which in all practical senses was one nation, maintained individual nation status for all its member states on the international level. The European Union was now the big kid on the block, and the one to which others bowed to gain favor. Even if the United States government and the United Nations were to have such influence over their European brothers, as Jim Allen hoped, they were not inclined to exercise it on behalf of the defense of Christians. Many legislators, some secretly, others openly, celebrated these new anti-blasphemy laws of Europe and began work to craft similar bills to present them before Congress.

Flexing its economic and political influence, the governing board of commissioners of the European Union, concerned with the uncensored nature of offensive material arriving by satellite or by the Global Web, presented to the United Nations a demand that all internationally accessible programming be strictly censored in terms of religiously inspired inflammatory teaching or comment. International law, especially in the area of communications, had developed sufficiently so that decisions made at the international level were of an obligatory nature. The proposal put forth by the European Union passed by an overwhelming margin, enjoying the support of the United States delegate. Within the next year, laws were passed in the United States strictly limiting the content of religious broadcasting. Christian web sites, publications, and television and radio stations suddenly had a whole new listening audience. Many of their new readers and listeners were determined to find violations of the law to be able to shut down their operations. Within a year and a half, 90% of Christian media was silenced either by exorbitant fines, which they could not pay, or the withdrawal of their publishing or broadcasting license.

Persecution of the Christian church in Muslim and Communist countries, left unchecked for lack of a public Christian voice and because of a Western culture now apathetic to its sufferings, advanced with a new fury and determination. Christians, and those who had simply been sympathetic to Christians and their message, were publicly disgraced, imprisoned, and killed in the most brutal of ways. Most of these stories never reached the press, as correspondents feared for their own lives and careers were they to comment on them in any way.

Though unaffected directly by the broadcast laws (Green Bluff Baptist Church didn't even have a web site), the enemies of the Gospel were emboldened by them, and made their presence felt in the small Wisconsin town. Articles began to appear in the commentary and opinion sections of the local Gazette, naming Jim and Green Bluff Baptist Church, and challenging them for their bigoted and hateful teaching. Due to the new laws, Jim had not even been able to use the same forum to respond publicly to these attacks.

A large homosexual group based in Milwaukee made the trip one Sunday to Green Bluff Baptist Church. Outnumbering the worshipers two to one, they harassed the believers on church grounds as they tried to enter the building. Many of the children, upset and scared by the protesters, were crying. Several of the church members attempted to witness to their adversaries, but their tracts were torn up in front of them, and their words were shouted down with chants of "bigots with Bibles, blasphemies and libels," and others of the like. Jim had been surprised by this attack. While opposed to homosexuality as a sin, Jim had never been a crusader on the issue and had often encouraged his congregation to love those who were enslaved by this and other rebellious lifestyles. "They aren't the enemies," he had said more than once. "They are victims of the enemy." Jim called the local police station, and was shocked when only two cars arrived and the police merely looked on as if spectators to the event. The minister of the United Church, hearing of the commotion, or perhaps having had something to do with the organizing of the protest, arrived with two other clergy members and attempted to serve as mediator. If Jim would only publicly affirm and celebrate homosexuality as one of the beautiful ways in which human love can be expressed, the protesters would turn into friends.

Families began to be absent from church events. Visiting them to see what might be the problem, Jim was openly attacked by some. He was misinterpreting the Bible and preaching lies to the congregation, they said. It was funny how they seemed to parrot the articles that had been written in the paper in opposition to Jim and the church. Others seemed honestly contrite. They wanted to be faithful to God, but expressed that they and their children had been under tremendous pressure from some of their neighbors to leave the church. In a couple of cases, the husbands confessed that they were told by their employers that they would be dismissed from their jobs if they continued to attend services. Their association with Green Bluff Baptist Church would "reflect badly on the company," they were told. Some wept as they confided to Jim the reasons that they were withdrawing membership, but few were persuaded to return. Jim saw average Sunday church attendance fall from 120 to 62.

Some of his former members became his most severe critics. The elder board met at one point, at the request of elders Sam Johansen and Ronald Smith, to vote on whether or not Jim should be allowed to continue on as pastor of the church. The meeting was long and heated, and at the end the vote was four to three in Jim's favor. The dissenting elders could have pushed the issue to a congregational vote, but decided not to. They attended one meeting following the vote. Sam Johansen broke into the prayer request time of the service to give a monologue about his family's long history in the church, and how the church had become the scandal and the laughingstock of the community. He finished by saying he would never withdraw his membership from the church, but neither would he set foot inside it again while Jim Allen was still pastor there. That said, he rose to leave the church. Others rose with him, but to his own surprise and fury his wife, Ellen, remained seated. He more or less commanded her to get up and leave with him, but she refused. She said in a weak but firm voice, "Pastor Jim has preached the gospel message just as Pastor Edgar did. He preaches the same message now as he did five years ago, when you, Sam, planned a surprise party in his honor, celebrating the blessing that his first five years as pastor had been to this church. I am not going to let godless men make me leave my church or abandon my faith, no matter what threats they might make, and no matter what ridicule I might have to endure. Jesus is my Lord and I will not deny Him." Tears had come to Jim's eyes, hearing this shy, normally submissive wife, stand up for her Lord. Sam, not to be left without the last word, stormed, "We'll see if your Jesus can put food in your mouth and a roof over your head." Then he fixed his eyes one last time on Jim and spoke very slowly, "You have turned my family against me, preacher man. I will not soon forget it." With that he turned and left the building. His children, a daughter, fifteen, and a son, seventeen, remained with their mother.

Chapter 4

As if God were pouring out His judgment on the nations for their attacks on His people, the world seemed to come loose at its seams. In a period of maybe eighteen months the world suffered catastrophes, mostly of human origin, as it never had before. War, always present in one area of the world or another, broke out, as if orchestrated, in all parts of the globe. The tribes of Africa, crossing national boundaries, rose up one against another in vicious slaughter. China and Taiwan, long at odds over issues of sovereignty, broke out into open warfare. North Korea, after years of feigned friendship, noting the distractions presented by the other battles, seized the opportunity and finally invaded South Korea. Indonesia, having calmed its internal disputes of previous years, broke forth into full scale civil war. The worst of the fighting occurred in the Persian Gulf area and Southern Asia. Old conflicts flared up between Iran and Iraq, with widespread use of biological and chemical weapons. India and Pakistan became the first nations to unleash the destructive power of nuclear weapons against one another. Syria, Jordan, Lebanon, and Palestine rose up anew against Israel, with other nations threatening to enter the fray. Border disputes, common for many years in South America, found new life, with the Peruvians and Venezuelans at the center of most of the conflicts. The Dominican Republic, tired of the illegal entry of the poorer Haitians into their territory because of the corruption of successive Haitian governments, invaded the western half of their island. Libya and Algeria struck out against their more moderate neighbors of Morocco, Tunisia, and Egypt. Unlikely battles erupted, such as a short lived Mexican military invasion along the southern Texas border. Many of these were spurred on by hunger, as a two-year-old drought caused desperate food shortages in many parts of the world. Terrorist groups, many with unknown goals and connections, began to strike, causing havoc and uncertainty among all, with Russia and the United States being their most common targets.

As a result of military and terrorist usage of biological weapons, the nuclear fallout from the war between Pakistan and India, and the drought conditions in many areas, previously unknown diseases, and diseases long since controlled or eradicated, broke forth in epidemic proportions. The medical and scientific communities worked at an exhausting pace, but they were fighting a losing battle. People were dying faster than they could be buried. In many cases, the bodies were bulldozed impersonally into mass graves.

Major earthquakes hit California, Mexico City, Tokyo, Turkey, Guatemala, Spain, and Italy leaving thousands dead and diverting relief efforts and supplies from other needy areas. Sickness, hunger, death, and chaos reigned. One of the estimates, which Jim read, said that as many as one fourth of the world's population had died in this eighteen month time period of apocalypse.

There was no part of the world left totally untouched. The one area of relative refuge from the disasters which had struck the world so hard and fast in those months were the countries of the European Union and their associate member nations. They were the only ones left with people and material resources beyond what they needed to deal with their own national tragedies. They were the only ones able to respond to the needs of the other nations surrounding them. The world was desperate and the nations looked to the Union for help.

In the midst of these monumental problems faced throughout the globe, a popular leader arose among the commissioners of the European Union. He had a charismatic personality which inspired confidence and loyalty. He made decisions with ease. His proposals seemed to offer real solutions. The others gave way to him, as he became first their spokesman and then their leader. He was propelled, not unwillingly, before the public. He appeared everywhere in the media. Thousands gathered to hear him every time he gave a speech. The texts of his addresses were printed in their entirety in most major news publications. It seemed as if his face appeared nightly on television screens throughout the world.

In the fall of 2018, the leaders of the European Union cloistered in a large estate outside of Prague to discuss and propose global solutions to the problems facing the world. They met for seven days. It was announced that on Monday, October 15 at 7:30 p.m. the decisions of the commissioners would be announced from Wenceslas Square in Prague. Every major news organization from Europe, as well as from other parts of the world, were there. The square was packed with some 125,000 onlookers. A large stage, with lights and loud speakers was set up in front of the National Museum. Security personnel prevented access to the platform. Others mixed in with the crowd or watched from surrounding roof tops. It was a cool, clear evening, and most of the crowd wore light jackets or sweaters. The light of the stars was obscured by the illumination in the square. The atmosphere was one of solemn expectation. No one was quite sure what to expect, but most felt sure that the proclamations to be made would directly affect not only the Union but the world.

Various world leaders had been invited to a five o'clock dinner, where they were briefed as to some of the decisions and announcements that were to be made that evening. In fact, they were hand picked leaders who had already been made aware two days earlier of the essence of the proposals to be put forth. Those present had given their initial consent and agreement to the core issues. Most of the leaders at the dinner represented countries that were already associate members of the Union, the idea being that they would be influential in carrying out the Union's desires in their own countries and regions. No press were present at the dinner and it was clarified beforehand that the leaders would remain in the banquet hall until the rally in the square was over, being witnesses to it by way of a large screen television link.

At 7:00 pm, flags, large and small, of the European Union were distributed among the vast crowd. Announcements were made over the loud speaker that no other banners would be permitted. On the stage itself, to the left and the right of a large blue and white European Union flag, were smaller flags representing all the countries of the world. In front of the flags were four chairs, two on either side of a crystal podium. This podium became the focal point of the square that evening. Above the flags had been placed large screens upon which the images of the speakers, and some of the text and slogans of their speeches would be projected. Selected satellite greetings from important leaders in other parts of the world would also be projected onto the screens.

At 7:25, military jets flew over the city and the loudspeakers began to play the European anthem.

At 7:30 sharp, a motorcade, surrounded by police motorcycles with their lights flashing and sirens blaring, approached the west side of the stage. A corridor had been roped off there and was lined with military personnel. It was 10:30 am Green Bluff time. In their living room, Jim and Sandy watched with great interest the events unfolding in Prague. Sensing that their life and ministry as a church body would somehow be directly influenced by the decisions made in Prague, the remaining faithful of Green Bluff Baptist Church had gathered for prayer the three previous evenings. They interceded fervently on behalf of the European leaders. They had not been sure exactly how to pray. "Thy will be done," seemed to be the unified petition, with the hope that the solutions presented would include a recognition of their errors in the persecution of Christians, and a renewed commitment to freedom for worship and witness. The small body had suffered much during the previous three years and were weary. At the same time, they knew their sufferings were nothing compared to those of their brethren in other parts of the world.

The four dignitaries who would take part in the presentation climbed to the platform, accompanied by the thunderous applause of the crowd. They spread out in the front part of the platform, waving to the crowd. After approximately ten minutes, three of the four took their places in their designated seats on the platform, and one, Germany's chancellor, took up position behind the podium. With much difficulty, he quieted the thunderous applause of the crowd and began his introduction. "We stand at a crucial moment in world history. We, the leaders of the European Union, in consultation with the United Nations, religious leaders, and the leaders of many of the great countries of the world, have been meeting over the past seven days to discuss the grave and multiple problems facing humanity, and to propose lasting solutions. At this moment, in the banquet hall of the Hotel Renaissance, are gathered the kings, presidents, and heads of government of many of the sovereign nations of the world. We have asked several of them, by satellite link, to give you greetings, following which Pope Adrian will bring greetings from St. Peter's Square. The Secretary General of the United Nations will then speak, outlining many of the problems facing our world that have brought us to this moment and to these measures, which we are convinced will usher us into a golden age of global prosperity and peace. We thank you for your presence here tonight and count on your full support as we move into this new age."

Several world leaders gave brief greetings. They stressed the grave problems facing the world and gave their appreciation to the European Union for being willing to address those problems. They spoke of having been briefed on the solutions to be presented that evening and expressed their full agreement and willingness to place the material and people resources of their nations at the disposal of the Union for the bringing about of peace and prosperity in the world.

While the European leaders were meeting in Prague, Pope Adrian VII had been meeting at the Vatican with religious leaders from throughout the world. The purpose of their gathering was to lend unified moral and religious support to the political solutions being offered in Prague. That very night, they were holding a parallel rally in Saint Peter's square. At 8:00, the Pope's greetings were beamed to the gathering in Prague. "Citizens of the world, we the leaders of the world's great religious faiths are gathered in St. Peter's Square. We are united in our anticipation and enthusiasm for the long awaited peace and unity for which we all have prayed. We are praying together for the realization of the unity of the nations as one and the end of religious division, hatred and distrust, which have sparked so many wars. We are ready to call one another brothers under the Fatherhood of God and denounce those who would claim an exclusiveness in relationship to Him. We are convinced that faith and politics must work together in unison, mutually supporting one another for the good of humanity. The moment is now if we are to have any hope of survival, and we are assured that God's chosen political instrument is the European Union. We therefore give full affirmation, lending our religious and moral authority to the European leadership. We call upon the faithful in all nations to work together for the furtherance of its goals. We cry out together, let there be unity and in unity, peace."

"Unity, and in unity, peace," flashed across the screens in Wenceslas Square.

The Secretary General of the United Nations rose to the platform.

"Let there be unity and in unity, peace. This has long been the goal of the United Nations, but our goal has been frustrated by the particular interests of our member nations. Nation has risen up against nation, and there has been no peace." He went on to name the various nations of the world, which in that very moment were at war with one another. "Terrorist organizations have prospered and caused havoc because of the lack of a unified action against them. They kill and they maim in one nation and simply cross the border to be safe in another. This cannot be. Citizens no longer feel safe in their own neighborhoods.

"Diseases have reached epidemic proportions. Our world's minds and resources are being wasted in unnecessary duplication of research efforts to find preventions and cures. Each nation and each research center competes against the other for the glory of being the first to find solutions and to market its products for profit. Instead of working together and sharing information and ideas there is market bred competition and secrecy. Meanwhile thousands are suffering and dying.

"It is estimated that in these last two years over one fourth of the world's population has died as a result of war, epidemic, or starvation. Sixty percent of the world's population is suffering from malnutrition. Fifty-five percent of these individuals are in danger of dying from starvation if food does not reach them soon." As the Secretary General spoke, images of war, sickness, starvation and death were projected on the screens behind him. "Is there a lack of food production that so many of our human brothers and sisters should be suffering? No. Mother Earth has provided us with abundant resources. Agricultural technology has made it possible to feed three times the present population of the world. The problem, as we all know it to be, is national and religious conflict and division. Speaking as its Secretary General, I declare to you that the United Nations has failed in its mission and become obsolete in terms of meeting the needs of today. We are in a desperate crisis. What we need is not the United Nations. We need a United Nation. We need a centrally governed world, in which the needs of all its inhabitants can be provided for and assured. The European Union has proved itself successful in the uniting of individual nations, many of whom had previously been at war one with the other, together as one nation.

It has proved its effectiveness in providing for the security and physical needs of its citizens. It has been bold in its addressing of religiously inspired bigotry and has led the world in its elimination. It has used its material resources in recent years, as no other nation has done, to alleviate the sufferings of others throughout the globe. It is the only political body in our world today that enjoys the level of respect and trust of other nations necessary to take the leading role in the formation of such a one world government. I am happy to say that in recent meetings the European Union has agreed to take on this challenge. We are grateful for the courage of its leaders. In an emergency meeting of the member nations of the United Nations to be held a week from next Saturday, I will propose that the United Nations, as it has existed, be abolished, and that its member nations yield their resources and their sovereignty to the European Union. It is a drastic measure, but it is the only one which offers hope for our planet and it is one which for many centuries our greatest thinkers have longed for. Let there be unity and let there be peace."

Across the screens flashed the slogans in the different languages of the world, "Let there be unity and let there be peace." "One world, one nation."

While the crowd gathered in Wenceslas Square and those watching throughout the world had expected to hear dramatic announcements and solutions to the problems facing the world, this announcement by the Secretary General of the United Nations was a shock The crowd was open mouthed as they looked one to the other. Jim in his home in Green Bluff put his head into his hands in disbelief and shock. He had known that this day would come, but he hadn't expected to see it. He was supposed to have been raptured before these things took place.

The European anthem began to blare again through the loud speakers. Many throughout the crowd unfurled their flags and waved them with great enthusiasm. Thousands of blue and white balloons were released from helicopters and the roof tops. The European flag was projected on to the large screens, alternately with the slogans, and the face of the fourth man now standing quietly on the stage. The crowd, reacting with stunned silence at first, broke forth in celebration, dancing, clapping and the chanting of, "Unity and Peace."

After some ten minutes of this, the third speaker approached the podium. He was the Prime Minister of England. After several minutes of trying, he was finally successful in quieting the crowd. "It is with great solemnity that I stand before you this night," he began. "As you have heard, the problems facing our world are great. I would be less than sincere with you if I were to say that as the leaders of the European Union we embrace wholeheartedly the proposal of forming a government that would encompass our globe-a Global Union. For the member nations of the European Union it will mean years of sacrifice and risk in order to try to bring the stability that we enjoy here to others. Selfishly, we discussed seriously the possibility of reducing rather than increasing our involvement in other parts of the world, but we have heard your cries. We have seen the sick and the dying. Pope Adrian and other religious leaders have reminded us of our moral responsibilities to humanity. We have come to agree with the Secretary General of the United Nations, that we alone are in a position to take on global leadership. We are now prepared to do so. We ask that the governments of the world and the citizens thereof cooperate fully with us. We ask that the governments of the world yield over their sovereignty to us for the greater good of their people and to the end of world peace. As prime minister, I will present to Parliament, as early as next week, a resolution that, with the dissolution of the United Nations, we as England cease to be in any sense a sovereign nation, in favor of full integration into a Global Union. Other European Union nations have promised to do the same.

"We call for an end to the wars between nations and commit our military forces, along with those of the countries who become one with us, against any acts of aggression.

"We give public warning to those contemplating acts of terrorism against innocent people. For the seriousness of the crime and its destabilizing effect on society, we have instituted a new law. Persons participating in acts of terrorism and those who would aid and abet terrorists will be publicly hanged. We are now living in difficult times, and difficult problems call for harsh solutions. If you commit a terrorist act, you will not be able to hide. We will find you and you will bear the consequences of your actions.

"We denounce religious bigotry as the source of many of the

world's conflicts. In order to avoid its bitter fruit, we must cut off this tree at its roots. Listen to me. Whether you call yourself a Christian, a Muslim, a Sikh, or a Jew, what right do you have to invent God and then to declare that your way is the only way to know Him? What right do you have to impose your beliefs on others? How many people have died throughout the centuries in the name of your God and your religion? The voices of those who rise up to proclaim that their beliefs are the only way to God will be silenced. The blasphemy of those who proclaim to be sinful those lifestyles which we as a society have declared to be legitimate will no longer be permitted. We have found the measures we have thus taken in Europe to be insufficient to eradicate these messages and messengers of hate. In those cases where guilt is proven or admitted, imprisonment will result. If it is proven over a period of time that the individual remains unrepentant, he or she will be beheaded. Society will not be forced to bear the cost over many years for those who refuse to live in accordance with its standards. We have spoken with Pope Adrian and the leaders of other religions, and they are in agreement that such measures, though unpleasant, are necessary. In consultation with the religious leaders now gathered in Rome, we have asked them, while permitting a degree of religious diversity and expression, that they formulate a focus of religious faith, that instead of dividing us would unite us together as the world's people. We seek unity and through unity, peace."

The slogans appeared once again on the screens, "Let there be unity and let there be peace," and, "One world, one nation." Interspersed with these appeared the European flag and the face of the fourth individual on the stage, who had yet to speak. The crowd waved its flags and the chant rose up, "Unity and Peace."

Quieting the crowd a second time, the Prime Minister of England continued. "Due to the multitude of problems facing us in the immediate future, we, the leaders of the European Union, have made a structural decision. We have agreed that many decisions in the coming days will need to be made decisively and quickly. The committee style by which the Union has functioned to this time is viewed as inadequate to address the multitude of crises that present themselves daily. The commissioners will continue to meet and aid in the decision processes, especially in their areas of expertise, but for an interim period we are asking one of the commissioners to step forward to function in the role of supreme leader. He will have full decision making authority to put into effect on a worldwide basis the ideals of the European community. His words will carry with them the full weight of law. Such responsibility is not lightly given. Were it not that we have in our midst one of exceptional intellect and ability, and one who deeply cares about the progress of humanity, we would not consider, even in these desperate times, putting such power in the hands of one man. In fact, as we the leaders of the European community have worked with him, we have noted superhuman abilities in him. He has our trust, and we know that he has yours as well. You have seen his face often in the last couple of years. You have benefitted by decisions that have had their origins in his mind and which have been carried to fruition as a result of his leadership. He is the right leader for these difficult times. We feel that if anyone can lead us into the unity and peace that we desire, it is he. You see him standing here before you. I present to you him whom you will now know as Supreme Leader of the European Union and of the world."

The Supreme Leader stepped forward to the podium to wild cheers of the crowd. He hugged the still Prime Minister of England, and presented himself before the people. The screens alternated between his person and the flag of the Union, as if the Union and he had now become one and the same. He began to silence the crowd, when suddenly a single shot rang out. The Supreme Leader raised his hands to the right side of his face and crumpled to the ground. In a moment's time he was shrouded by security personnel. But it was too late. The Supreme Leader had been shot.

Chapter 5

What happened next has to be understood in the context of the political terrorism that had taken place during the previous two years. Memories were still fresh concerning the blood bath that had occurred in the United States in 2016 at a Republican presidential political rally held in Austin, Texas. Somehow avoiding or infiltrating security measures at the event, a group of at least twelve terrorists, armed with explosive devices and automatic weapons, turned the rally into a war zone. Eight hundred and twenty people lost their lives in a matter of four or five minutes, with thousands of others being injured.

At seeing the Supreme Leader shot, the crowd gathered at Wenceslas Square panicked. The next ten minutes were utter bedlam. What had been an orderly rally turned into riot. People began to flee in all directions, pushing and trampling one another in their desperate attempt to escape. The security forces present, though great in number, found themselves helpless before the hysterical waves of humanity. In fear, or in some misguided attempt to halt the onrush of bodies, some fired their weapons into the air. Instead of calming the situation, it added to the panic and the conviction on the part of those present that they must escape the square as quickly as possible or be annihilated.

On the stage, efforts were being made to attend to the immediate needs of the Supreme Leader, who lay motionless in a pool of his own blood. A stretcher was brought from the motorcade area, but it was impossible, for the moment, to safely move him from the area. After several minutes, a helicopter arrived, and made several attempts to land. Finally, it was successful, and the Supreme Leader was quickly placed inside. The helicopter took off in the direction of the city's best hospital.

Jim had sat numbly in front of the television set as the commentators droned on about the events occurring in Prague. No, the security personnel did not know who had shot the Supreme Leader or the motive behind it. No, there had not been any other terrorist acts perpetrated in the Square that they were aware of, though many were dead and hundreds injured because of the panic which ensued following the shot. Correspondents reported from the hospital as to the possible condition of the newly declared Supreme Leader. Those who knew weren't saying, but that did not stop the unending speculation which so often follows events such as these. Medical experts from throughout the globe were interviewed as to what damage might have occurred. The image of the moment of impact was shown again and again. Emphasis was placed on the fact that, after the initial response of the hands to the head and his fall to the ground, the Supreme Leader had not moved. This indicated serious damage. Terrorist experts were brought forth. In their opinion, who might have fired the shot? In a moment, with the pull of one trigger, the dramatic content of the announcements made in Wenceslas Square that evening were swallowed up in concern for the well-being of the Supreme Leader.

Jim's watching was interrupted several times by phone calls from the faithful. They had not missed the content! Their concern was not so much for the Supreme Leader, as it was for themselves and their families. Would they be put in prison and perhaps beheaded? Jim had tried to be persuasive, assuring them that they lived in the United States, and that these announcements would not affect them. Surely the United States government would not give over its sovereignty to the European Union. It was difficult to comfort with these words, however, for Jim himself had many doubts as to their truth. He had thought to comfort by saying that God would protect them. These were no doubt the end times, and Jesus would return for His church before they would suffer tribulation. He thought better of it, though, for he was no longer sure of these words which he had preached so many times. Had they not already suffered greatly? He agreed with elder Svensen, that those remaining loyal to the church needed to meet that night to discuss and pray about the things they had heard that morning. Jim would make the calls, and they would meet at 8:00 in the church sanctuary.

At Sandy's urging, they turned off the television at about 1:00 pm. They ate lunch together, and Jim went to his office to make the calls to his congregation and to be alone with his Lord. Behind the closed door of his office, Jim poured out his soul before the Lord. It might properly be called a gripe session. Jim recalled to the Lord all the difficulties they had gone through in the previous couple of years as a community, a church and a family. He reminded the Lord that he had been faithful to preach His Word and to live a godly life. He cried out in repentance of sins known or unknown. He reviewed with the Lord the events of that very day and the threats against the Gospel put forth in the speeches from Prague. He argued with God as to the way the events were unfolding. "What about the rapture of your church, Lord?" He thought of those who were suffering more. He prayed for the Sam Johansen family. He prayed for his brothers and sisters in Christ living in Europe. For them there would be no time to make plans. He prayed and he prayed until he entered into an exhausted sleep.

He awoke at 5:15, knees stiff and sore. He thought about the meeting that night and jotted down some ideas. It seemed to him, that as much as preparing for the rapture, they needed now to prepare for persecution. Before leaving his office, he thought to call the pastor of the Trinity Evangelical Lutheran Church. Jim had pastored longer in Green Bluff than his counterpart, but Rev. Peter Samuels had been in the ministry for a longer time, having served in four pastorates prior to his move to Green Bluff five years earlier. Their acquaintance had grown into a friendship and then a true brotherhood. They were the only pastors in the immediate area who had remained true to biblical teaching and proclamation, and they had suffered for it. Being a more traditional church in its form of expression and worship, and Pastor Samuels more staid and cautious by nature than Jim, the brunt of the attacks fell to Jim and the Green Bluff Baptist Church. Pastor Samuels, however, was not a man of compromise and did not fear to take biblical stands. It had been he who first called Jim following Jim's blowup with his elders. It had been he who first encouraged Jim to stand strong following the church's confrontation with the homosexual protesters. Not only did Pastor Samuels encourage Jim in private, he also publicly supported his stands for righteousness. Six months earlier the two had decided to meet each Friday morning at 7:00 am for prayer. Jim dialed Rev. Samuel's home.

Paul Nilsen

The phone was picked up on the second ring. Jim remembered the conversation clearly.

"Hello, Peter?"

"Jim," Peter responded, "I'm so glad to hear your voice. You must be aware of what has been taking place today. Jim, I'm so excited. You were right. You were right! We must be in the end times. The commentators are saying that the Supreme Leader will not make it through the night. But they're wrong, Jim. They're wrong! I'm convinced now that he is the antichrist that you said would come, and which I now see the Bible foretold. Jim, this is Revelation 13:3. The Supreme Leader has received a mortal wound to the head, but somehow he will be healed."

Jim was shocked. Pastor Samuels had always held to a post-millennial view of end time events, where Christ's return would be ushered in by the triumphal church's moral and spiritual conquest of the world. He had often chided Jim for being pessimistic as to the present and future state of the world. True, he had struggled during those years of suffering, trying to maintain his optimism in the face of the worldwide persecution of the church and the apparent abandoning of the faith on the part of many who had previously professed Christ. Still, he had not believed in the rapture of the church, spiritualizing and placing in a past historical context the verses which made reference to such an event. Jim had to make sure he was talking to the right person.

"Hello, am I talking to Peter Samuels, pastor of the Evangelical Lutheran Church?" Jim asked again.

"Yes, yes, Jim. Stop joking. After watching the announcements made in Prague, and seeing the shooting of the Supreme Leader, I've been holed up in my office, reading again and again the end time passages of which you so often made mention. I've read Matthew 25. I've read Luke 21. I've read First and Second Thessalonians. I've read Second Peter. If you can believe it, I've read through Revelation four times this afternoon. The whole book! Jim, you're right. I don't know how I didn't see it before. Of course there is a rapture of the church, and it's coming soon."

"Your confidence is greater than mine now, I'm afraid," Jim replied. "The rapture ought to have occurred by now. Christ's church was not appointed for such suffering as we're going through. Read

42

First Thessalonians 5:9, 'God has not appointed us for wrath...' Look at Second Thessalonians 2:6-8. The wicked one will not be revealed until the Holy Spirit is removed from the scene with the church in the rapture. Look at Revelation. The church isn't mentioned after chapter 3, and all the calamities occur following that chapter. If it weren't for the fact that I know others who are still here, and who will surely be raptured when the rapture takes place, I would think that it had already occurred and that I had been left behind. Now I don't know what to think."

"Jim, do not lose faith. Your people need you now more than ever. I was guilty of seeing what I wanted to see in the Bible. You're guilty now of the same thing. You're trying to make those verses say what they do not say, and it's causing you doubts. Read the passages over again. You will see clearly that the church will experience world-wide persecution, as we are experiencing it now, before Jesus comes to take us to be with Him. It's one of the clearest signs. It's what has caused me to change my view of the end times. It's hard, Jim, but it's exciting. Jesus is coming back soon, but there is likely to be great suffering before he does. We may need to lay down our lives for Him. Read the passages again, Jim. Read them without a prejudiced mind. You haven't missed the rapture, Jim. It isn't a lie. It's coming. Be encouraged."

They talked for a few minutes longer. As he hung up, Jim thought to himself, "Read the passages again...without prejudice." He practically knew them all by heart. And yet, he could not deny the events taking place around him.

At home, before the meeting, Jim tuned into the news to see how events had progressed. He wanted to be as up to date as possible for the church meeting that night. Besides, it was difficult for him to think of anything else. The news confirmed what Rev. Samuels had said on the phone. Although medical terms escaped Jim, the clear prognosis for the Supreme Leader was imminent death. Damage was such that they had ceased, after many hours, to try to intervene surgically. They kept him heavily medicated to try to avoid any pain he might be in and were standing by for his last breath. They had sent word to Pope Adrian, asking him to come and pronounce last rites over him. Pope Adrian was at that moment on his way from the Vatican to Prague.

What was more shocking, was that guilt for the shooting was being placed on right wing radical Christians, angry over the European Community's efforts of previous years to control their sectarian teachings. A phone call had been received by the supposed shooter, laying claim to the act, and referring to the Union's having taken away his children. He threatened other acts of violence and assured that he was not acting alone. There was a large network of righteously angry followers of Christ who would be going to war against the godless Union. The phone call had been recorded, and was played over and over again throughout the newscast. Although there was no corroborating evidence to back the claim of the caller, his words were being taken as fact. A call was made to all citizens of the Union to report to their local authorities the presence of any family members or neighbors who belonged to this dangerous sect. Raids had already taken place on the homes of some of these radicals, and it was reported that rifles and hand guns had been found in several of the locations. Jim wept as he watched many of his brothers and sisters being dragged off to prison for the terrible crime of professing Christ Jesus as Lord.

Chapter 6

The events snowballed from there.

First, there was the church meeting. The group that met was smaller than anticipated. When he had made the phone calls to the faithful earlier that day, Jim had noticed that several of them seemed to be looking for a way out of being present that night. Jim had encouraged them as to the importance of this meeting. They seemed frightened; with good reason, Jim had thought at the time.

Ellen Johansen and her children were there. They had been kicked out of their home by Sam the night of the explosive congregational meeting and had been living with the Svensens since that time. God had indeed provided a roof over their heads and food in their stomachs.

Elder Svensen and Elder Brown were there with their wives and families.

John Brown, an elderly bachelor, was there.

Cindy Allerton, Pam and Peter Green, and John Stiles, all young adults who had accepted Christ several years earlier through the youth ministry of the church, were present.

There were a couple of teenagers there, Paul Stiles and his friend Peter Olsen. John and Paul's parents were indifferent to the gospel, feeling themselves to be good and moral people. They had seen, however, that the church had a positive effect in their sons' lives and were glad to have them participate in the life of the church. Even in recent years, when the persecution had been so great, they supported the decision that their sons had made to follow Christ. Peter Olsen was rather new to the church. Jim had thought that he attended more for his interest in one of the Brown girls than for his interest in Christ, but for whatever reason, there he was.

The Wisniewski and Chetnik families were there. They were the two Catholic families who had left the Catholic Church years earlier because of its flip-flop on moral issues. Arriving at Green Bluff Baptist Church, they were confronted with a different message than what they had been taught all their lives, but it was one that attracted them. When presented with the simplicity of the gospel message, they eagerly responded. Soon after, they confessed their faith in Christ through baptism and had been active members of the church body ever since.

The Jeremiah Brown family was there.

Sherry MacClennon, a divorced mother, and her two young children were there.

To Jim's surprise, at about 8:05, Ronald Smith walked in and quietly sat down.

They were waiting for others to arrive when Ronald Smith stood up. "I know that it is a surprise for most of you to see me here tonight," he began. "I'm not sure how he found out about this meeting, but Sam Johansen called me up about it around 6:00 pm. He said that he would be making calls to the church congregation, warning you of and threatening you with the announcements made this day in Prague. I imagine that most of you received such a call." Many of those present nodded their heads in agreement with this statement. "There are many who are not present here, whom I imagine also received such calls. Sam wanted once again that I should be his ally in tearing down this church and the cause of Christ. I'm here instead to ask your forgiveness. I could make up excuses for my actions, but what it boils down to is that I denied my Lord. Under pressure from Sam, from my wife, from my employer, and from my neighbors, I denied my Lord. I failed Him and I failed you. I ask for your forgiveness. To tell you the truth, Sam asked me to do just what I'm doing now. He asked me to feign repentance to infiltrate this group as a spy. I'm sorry to have to say this Ellen, but he's an enemy of Christ and of all you who would follow Him. God help him, he will do everything he can to destroy you. As for me, I've asked my Lord's forgiveness and I pray that God will grant me the grace to die confessing Jesus as my Savior and Lord. Thank you my friends for not denying Him as I did."

With that Ronald rose and exited the room. Curiously, no one moved to encourage him to stay.

Elder Svensen rose after an awkward pause, stating that it was he who had asked that the meeting be called. He recalled to the congregation the prayer vigil that they had concerning the decisions of the European Union. He updated all those present concerning the events and announcements of that day. He emphasized the persecution of their Christian brothers and sisters in Europe at that very moment. Surely the persecution would spread to America and to Green Bluff. How should they as a church respond?

"Can we turn back the tide?" asked Donald Chetnik.

This was discussed for some 15 minutes. It was generally agreed that they had done what they could. The Christian public voice had been silenced. The national and international organizations no longer defended their rights but rather stood in opposition to the gospel. How should they pray? Should they pray for revival and a spiritual transformation of the culture? Most agreed that the prayer focus should now be faithfulness on the part of the believers, come what may.

"What about the rapture?" asked Jeremiah Brown.

Jim spoke at this point. "You know how I've preached to you the second coming of Jesus Christ. I've proclaimed that those who accepted Christ would not suffer the tribulation which would come upon the earth. Instead, it seems as if we are the focal point of it. I preached it because I believed it with all my heart. I don't know how to explain to you what is happening. I never expected the church to see the unveiling of the antichrist. I never expected we would suffer as we are suffering now. I confess to you that I am no longer sure what to believe regarding the rapture. I am sorry if I've given you false hope."

Peter Olsen, bold by nature, raised his hand for permission to speak. "I'm new here, and I don't know much about church meetings, but I'd like to say something. I don't know about all of you, but I didn't receive Jesus as my Savior and Lord in order to avoid suffering. With all due respect, you'd have to be nuts to do that. My life was a whole lot easier before knowing Christ. Every time I come here I have a battle with my folks. I'm brainwashed, you know. I answer back that I'm also soul washed by the blood of Jesus. It's amazing, but they preferred it when I was sneaking out to take drugs. I accepted Jesus as my Lord because He is God and because He died for me. I gave my heart to Jesus. I suspect he can have my head too, if it comes to that. By the way, I'd like to be baptized."

His words were like a bright light cutting through the darkness. It was the newest believer who brought encouragement to a very battle weary group. Had it not been for his words, it is very possible that the church would have decided to withdraw into itself for protection sake and, if possible, preservation. Instead, with fear and trembling, they agreed that they must continue to be a light, come what may, in the very dark moment of history in which they were living. They would continue to hold public meetings. They would continue to proclaim Christ. They would welcome all who would come to hear, not questioning the motives they might have for attending. It was not an easy decision to make, but the only other option available to them was that of denying their Lord by failing to be His witnesses.

Following the meeting, Jim placed a call to Ronald Smith and asked him to come back as an active member of the congregation.

Second, there was the miraculous healing of the Supreme Leader. Peter Samuels' words proved to be prophetic. Rising the following morning, Jim turned on the radio to the news that the Supreme Leader had been miraculously healed through the agency of Pope Adrian. Jim immediately went to the living room and turned on the television set. It was on every channel. With the arrival of Pope Adrian, select television crews had been allowed into the hospital room where the Supreme Leader had lain in a coma. Jim watched with interest what had taken place some two hours earlier. The cameras focused in on the Supreme Leader. Tubes came out from him in every direction. They showed as the Pope entered the room, dressed in his clerical robes. Amazingly, before directing his attention to the Supreme Leader, he looked directly into the television cameras. Motioning to the nearby bed, he proclaimed, "This is the terrible result of religious intolerance and bigotry at its worst. Little groups of little men with little minds have contrived to deprive our world of the peace and unity we long for. They say they have the only way." He again motioned towards the bed. "This is their way. They have tried to eliminate the one who would lead us into the new age for which we yearn, but their hatred will not succeed." Drawing near the bed in which the Supreme Leader lay, the Pope crossed himself, muttered some inaudible words, sprinkled holy water over the Supreme Leader's body, placed a dab of it upon his bandaged head, and raised the Leader's hand and kissed it. Then, before the cameras and before the strangely silent doctors present in the room, Pope Adrian did the unimaginable. He began to remove the bandages from the head of the Supreme Leader. More properly said, he removed the bandages from what remained of the head. The bullet had been one which exploded on impact. A significant portion of the skull had been blown away, as if sheared off by a sword. Not knowing of guns and bullets, the Apostle John could not have described the injury suffered by the Supreme Leader with any greater accuracy. The gray of the brain tissue could be clearly seen in several places, along with the reddish brown of dried blood. It was amazing that the doctors still declared the Supreme Leader to be alive.

"Look what you have done," Pope Adrian spoke again into the cameras. "Look at what those who say that their God is the only God, or that their interpretation of a particular religion is the only right interpretation, have done."

There was not even an effort at diplomacy on the part of Pope Adrian. It was a full frontal assault against Jim and those like him.

Pope Adrian turned again to his strange and inexplicable work. He began disconnecting the machines and tubes to which the Supreme Leader was attached. It was as if he had decided that the Supreme Leader was dead and now had no need of the machinery. When all life support systems had been removed, Pope Adrian again turned to the cameras. He spoke using biblical terminology. "The forces of evil have meant this for harm, but God has meant it for good. As Jesus asked that the stone be removed away from Lazarus' tomb, so have I released your Supreme Leader from that which had bound him." He lifted his eyes to the ceiling and raised his hands upward. "Father, I thank you that you have heard me. I know that you always hear me, but because of the people who watch, I have said it, that they may know me as the messenger and the Supreme Leader as their earthly lord." Turning again towards the bed, he laid his hands on the injured area and spoke. "Live and be healed."

He removed his hands. Visibly, before the cameras, apart from any other intervention medical or otherwise, the wound began to heal. The indentation of the skull grew outward. The shattered particles drew together covering over the brain cavity. It was unbelievable, and yet there it was happening. Was the whole thing being staged somehow, or was it true? Jim knew that it was true, and that the Father to whom Pope Adrian had spoken was the devil. After several moments, the Supreme Leader began to stir. Moans came from deep within him. His body rolled. His right hand went to the place where he had been shot.

"Clean him," Pope Adrian directed. The doctors and nurses, stunned by what they were seeing, made no move. "Clean him," repeated the Pope. Two of the doctors drew near. They examined the area where the wound had been, consulting in low voices one with the other. "It's a miracle," they exclaimed, turning to Pope Adrian and proclaiming the obvious. "It's a miracle!"

"Clean him," the Pope repeated for the third time.

The doctors called for the antiseptics and gauze and carefully cleaned the area. The Supreme Leader opened his eyes and smiled. He said in a quizzical, almost conversational tone, "What is this? What am I doing here?"

The doctors parted as Pope Adrian drew near him once again. "Welcome back, Your Excellence. Would you like to sit up?" The Supreme Leader sat up and faced the cameras. There was what looked like extensive scar tissue where the wound had been, but there was no opening and no blood now.

"Behold the man," declared the Pope. "If you will now excuse yourselves, the Supreme Leader needs to rest, and the doctors will need to confirm his health. If you please..." With those words closed the television coverage of what had taken place in the hospital room in Prague, and the commentators entered into their spin about the incredible events that had taken place.

In the months that followed, led by a very alive, very energetic Supreme Leader, the plans of the European Union which they had announced in Prague became an increasing reality. The United Nations Security Counsel, after heated debate, suspended some of its normal rules and presented to its member nations the proposal put forth by the Secretary General. The proposal read: "The United Nations, with the majority vote of its member nations, will cease to exist as a political body, and will cede over to the European Union its property and resources, to be better used in meeting the needs of the world's people." It was a power play, pure and simple. The member and associate nations of the European Union pushed the measure against the opposition of some of the larger, still proud, and in some cases prosperous nations, such as Russia, China, and Japan. The European nations and their allies carried the day. The United States, apparently reluctant to offend either the Union or the nations that stood opposed to the measure, abstained. The nations of southern Africa decimated by war, famine, and disease and dependent on the economic help that they had been receiving from the Union, voted in favor of the proposition. The South American Spanish speaking nations, with the exception of Peru and Venezuela, voted in favor as well, and for similar reasons. A time period of three months was set in which the leadership of all UN agencies and the transfer of all UN properties would be yielded over to the European Union. An exception was made for those properties which were located in countries which had been opposed to the dissolution of the United Nations. In such cases, the property was transferred back into the hands of the government of the country in which the property was located.

Within two weeks of the United Nations vote, the member and associate nations of the European Union renounced any claim to individual sovereignty and pledged full allegiance to the Union and to the Supreme Leader as the head thereof. The European Union, as such, ceased to exist. Its name was changed to the Global Union, to better reflect its new, expansive nature. A commission was formed by which other nations would be admitted into the Union. Applications flooded in.

The "Global Force of Peace" wasted no time in implementing the will of the Supreme Leader. The combined military force of the Global Union, its intelligence resources, and its access to bases throughout the world, made it the most powerful military unit ever to exist on the face of the earth. The Supreme Leader plainly and openly declared that any government or terrorist organization that persisted to perpetuating armed conflict would be dealt with harshly, and that its leaders would be held personally responsible. He backed up his words with the full military might of the Union. In a matter of six months, wars had ceased and the rumors of war were silenced. In some cases warring factions, out of fear, voluntarily laid down their weapons. In other cases, armies of warring nations were simply squashed in offensives that made the German blitzkrieg of World War II look slow.

Military intervention was not the Force's only role. As peace was established throughout the world, they turned their attention, with the help of thousands of civilian workers, to the distribution of food and medical supplies. Now, such resources were actually reaching the needy, who were, in turn, put to productive tasks as their abilities allowed and their regional demands required. Natural disasters were responded to with speed and efficiency. Thousands continued to die in epidemics, but now they were being cared for during their last hours of life in hospitals and clinics, even in the most rural areas of the world.

The Global Union and the Supreme Leader proved efficient and effective in their response to world needs.

They also demonstrated their efficiency in the execution of the other proposals put forth in Prague. Christians who lived in what was now the Global Union were arrested on a massive scale. They were sentenced to three months of intensive indoctrination in which time they had the opportunity to renounce their faith in Jesus Christ as the only mediator between God and man. At the end of the three months time, should it take that long, a document was placed before the prisoner to be signed. It read, "God, should He/She exist, has manifested Him/Herself through all the world's greater and lesser religions. I hereby acknowledge, affirm, and celebrate the faith of all men, and renounce as false my previous belief in Jesus alone as Savior and Lord. I furthermore affirm the sacred books of all religions and renounce as false my previous belief in the Bible as the exclusive Word of God. I hereby agree not to promote or impose my beliefs or lifestyle as being superior to those of anyone else, and will expose to the authorities those individuals that would continue in this error." There was a similar document that was presented to those who clung to other faiths as being the absolute truth. Following the three month time period, the individuals who refused to sign the document were publicly beheaded. Through the news programs, Jim had been witness to many of these beheadings and had given thanks to God for those who remained faithful to Christ unto death. There were those, however, who, amidst the applause and congratulations of the godless, did renounce their faith. It was a time where "brother" turned against brother, and family members turned one against the other. Christians became wary of one another, not being sure if they were talking with a friend or a traitor.

Before and after Canada's official entry into the Global Union, many Canadian Christians crossed the border into the United States for refuge from extermination. Green Bluff Baptist Church became a refugee center for a time. Pews were moved aside as the sanctuary became the men's dormitory and the fellowship hall the women's residence. Oh how alive the church was during those days! It was a blessing not only to the Canadian believers to have a place to stay, but it helped the remaining members of the church in Green Bluff to have a new focus and get their minds off their own difficulties. Believers came and went as they traveled on to other parts of the United States or found apartments in which to live. Under pressure from the Global Union, however, Congress began discussing the repatriation of such religious refugees to the Union. A week before the vote, anticipating what was to come, Jim, with the support of the elders of the church, closed the church down as a center for receiving and helping their fellow believers. That is not to say that they stopped helping. In an operation similar to the underground railroad in slavery days, the members of Green Bluff Baptist Church, along with other groups in the United States, set up a series of safe houses and routes by which the former Canadians could travel safely from one place to another. Jim had stood many times exactly where he was now standing with brothers and sisters in Christ who were fleeing the Global Union. It was one of the meeting places along what they had called "Jacob's Ladder." Only now, it was Jim who was on the run.

Chapter 7

It was three months earlier, following the signing into law of the "Unity and Acceptance of Faith Act" by the President, that Tom Watson first urged Jim to move out of Green Bluff for the sake of his family. He could move to an area where he and his preaching were not known, and he would be in less danger. He could continue to give testimony of his faith in Jesus if he must, but on a careful, individual basis that might not land him in prison. In Green Bluff, he was the pastor, the earthly figurehead of the church. The authorities would come for him first. Maybe if he left, they would overlook the other members of the congregation and let them be.

Jim had given serious consideration to Tom's reasoning but had been reluctant to make such a drastic move at that time. He decided to wait awhile and see how things played out. Many times, he knew, laws had been established to placate one group or another, without any serious intent on the part of the government to enforce the laws. He also knew that Wisconsin's governor was a professed believer in Jesus Christ, and Jim felt sure that he would in no wise enforce such harsh and freedom crushing legislation.

Jim's hopes that the new law might not be implemented were quickly dashed. As with everything else that had happened in recent years, the law was acted on with lightning speed. In the first month of the new law, it became obvious that, indeed, the national government was serious about the enforcement of its decree. Believers in many states of the union were arrested and jailed. Taking their cue from the Global Union, those who were imprisoned were released, free of charges, at any hearing in which they would deny their faith. Those who refused to do so were sentenced to two-year jail terms. Such terms apparently would be recurring upon release, were one to continue to hold to and propagate the hateful and divisive doctrines of sectarianism. Jim read of accounts where in several states police and National Guard units had surrounded church

Paul Nilsen

buildings while the believers were inside holding worship services. A tribunal, of sorts, was set up on the spot. Those present were asked a few brief questions. "Do you believe that faith in Jesus Christ is the only way to heaven? Do you believe that the Bible is the authoritative Word of God? Do you believe that those who break the commandments given in the Bible are sinners?" There were only two optional answers, yes or no. It was made clear ahead of time that those who answered "yes" to any of the three questions would be jailed. Those who answered "no" to all three questions were allowed to go free, with a warning against associating with such criminals in the future.

The prison system, in a matter of days, was overwhelmed. Detention camps had to be hastily constructed in order to house the new detainees. A debate arose as to the cost of housing and feeding these hundreds of thousands of new prisoners. It was impossible that society would be able to bear up under the financial strain of maintaining them over an extended period of time. The options appeared limited. They could: (1) Convince the new prisoners to renounce their beliefs, thus freeing up prison space. In the experience of the Global Union, this option had met with little success. Even with the real threat of being publicly beheaded, only 40% of those who were imprisoned because of their religious convictions renounced their faith. (2) They could repeal or change the law. (3) They could decide for capital punishment for those who remained unrepentant. Even as Jim stood overlooking Green Bluff, these latter two options were being debated heatedly in all sectors of society, and it seemed unclear which opinion would carry the day.

There were several instances where the implementation of the law was met with armed resistance. Some Christian groups, seeing the coming storm, had stockpiled weapons and food. Their goal was not to go out and create havoc in society, nor to begin a second American revolution or civil war. They were, however, determined that they would fight to protect their families. They would not be dragged off to prison peacefully for that which, in their minds and convictions, was no crime. Many of these like minded people had banded together in isolated areas. Confrontation by law enforcement officials had ended in bloody conflict. Many of these little wars continued and were used by the media to demonstrate the importance

56

of the new law and the need to rid society of those with intolerant religious views.

Seeing the seriousness with which the law was being implemented in other states, Jim and Sandy made the decision that Sandy and the children would go back to the farm to stay with her folks for the time being. They would be safer there. Jim had visited there three times and frequently talked with Sandy and the children over the telephone. He missed holding Sandy in his arms and her ever encouraging, down-to-earth counsel. The kids, unaware of the seriousness of the situation, were having a great time with their grandparents. They loved to run through the pastures and to help grandpa with the cows. Jim had been glad for their happiness. He grieved knowing that that happiness would now end.

Some eighteen states resisted implementing the "Unity and Acceptance of Faith Act." Wisconsin was one of them. Governor Graham stood firm against protest groups from within the state and against threats issued by the federal government. Religious intolerance was not a problem in his state, he affirmed again and again, and he would not permit that individuals be imprisoned on the basis of their religious convictions. Sincere Christians, Jews, and Muslims did not present a threat to society. Society benefitted by their moral influence and their service to their communities.

Jim rejoiced at the strength of Governor Graham's stand on the issue but wondered how long he would be able to withstand the pressure being placed upon him. The answer was not long in coming. Two months following the signing of the "Unity and Acceptance of Faith Act," those governors who refused to implement the federal law were threatened with removal from office and imprisonment. In South Carolina, this threat was met with force. Federal agents were escorted to the state's border by National Guard units and the borders were secured. The governor, surrounded by National Guard personnel at the state capital, extended a personal invitation to all Bible believing Christians to come and find refuge in the beautiful state of South Carolina. "As your passport into the state, bring your Bible. To help in the defense of your God given right of freedom of conscience and faith, bring your gun." Was he trying to bluff the Federal Government, or was he serious? Would South Carolina really go to war against the rest of the country?

Governor Graham did not enjoy such committed support for his views in Wisconsin, nor did he share the vision of armed resistance which he knew would be a losing battle. His speech to the Wisconsin people was more resigned than defiant. "Fellow citizens of Wisconsin, I have enjoyed the privilege of serving as your governor during the last six years. It is a privilege which I fear will soon come to an end. The federal government has threatened to remove me from office within the next twenty days for my refusal to implement federal law in our great state of Wisconsin. As long as I am governor, "The Unity and Acceptance of Faith" law will not be applied in Wisconsin. It is a law which goes against my principles and against the history and spirit of these United States. Good citizens throughout our country have been and are being imprisoned for the crime of believing in absolute truth and in a God who has revealed Himself to humanity in concrete ways. Though it will cost me my job and no doubt my freedom, I declare myself to be one of them. I have not hidden my Christian faith in the past, and I will not deny it now. While I have opportunity, I wish to thank you, the good people of Wisconsin, for your confidence and support. I will continue to serve you, as circumstances permit."

Faithful to their word, the federal government, at the end of twenty days, moved into the state capital backed by the force of the United States military. The governor met them on the steps of the capitol building. Offering no resistance, he was removed from office under charges of failing to fulfill his oath of office and was arrested for violating the "Unity and Acceptance of Faith" law.

It was that same day that Tom had phoned Jim, once again urging him as a friend to leave the area. Still Jim resisted. Perhaps it was because of an over developed sense of duty; perhaps he simply hated to flee before the threats of a bully (Jim wasn't quite sure himself), but he refused run. His flock was in danger and he, as their chosen shepherd, needed to be there to encourage them to be faithful to their Lord. Tom was not to be put off easily. To placate him, Jim agreed to an emergency plan of escape for when arrest was imminent. Tom, should he become aware of an arrest order against Jim, would call him. Jim would flee immediately and they would meet in the remote place where Jim now stood. It was a place that they both knew well. Tom and Jim had spent many hours together fishing for northern pike in the nearby lake. For Jim it was a favorite area to walk with the family or to walk alone and pray to his heavenly Father.

Sam Johansen also phoned Jim that day. His voice was as menacing as his message. "We're coming for you," Sam hissed. "Your days are numbered. When you're out of the way, maybe things can return to the way they ought to be around here. I told you I wouldn't forget what you did to my family. I just hope I'm there when they slap on the handcuffs. It won't be long and we'll be rid of you."

How difficult were the teachings of God's Word. "Give thanks in all circumstances." "Rejoice always." "Pray for those who persecute you." The words were somewhat forced, but nonetheless, Jim had kneeled and prayed, "Lord thank you for these threats. Thank you for the "Unity and Acceptance of Faith Law." I don't understand it, Lord, and I fear for what the future holds, but I acknowledge, Lord, that you know all about this situation. May your will be done. Give me your heart of love for Sam Johansen. Work in his heart a spirit of repentance and faith. Allow him to know the joy of your salvation. Lord, if I should be imprisoned or even put to death for your sake, give me the strength to be faithful to You to the end."

Chapter 8

Jim looked at his watch. It was 4:30 in the afternoon. The sun was beginning its descent over his shoulder, and the shadows were growing longer. How peaceful the town looked from where he sat.

Several cars passed on the winding road below. Jim was relieved to note that none of them were police cars. At 5:15, Jim saw what he had been waiting to see. The blue Ford Escort of his friend Tom Watson was making its way up to the agreed upon meeting point. Jim immediately scrambled down the hill on which he was standing and made his way through the underbrush to his car. Tom pulled his car off the road almost directly behind where Jim had parked. Jim arrived at the door before Tom had a chance to open it.

"I'm glad to see you here, Jim," Tom said, exiting his car. "I thought maybe they had gotten to you before you made it out of the house. Where's your car?"

"It's right here!" Jim quipped. Tom's presence always made Jim feel more at ease...even a bit boyish. It was one of the things that he valued about their friendship.

"You're an outlaw and now your driving invisible cars."

"I'd be safer if I did," Jim replied. "Look, it's over there."

Tom squinted his eyes in the direction in which Jim pointed. "You've hid it well. I've brought something else to help disguise it a little." Opening the trunk of his car, Tom removed two Wisconsin license plates.

"What are you going to do with those?" Jim asked.

"You're new at this fugitive business, aren't you? The police have an order out for your arrest. They know what your license plate number is. If we exchange these with yours, it might just throw them off your trail for awhile." That said, Tom removed a screw driver from his tool box and went over to Jim's car to make the switch. While Tom worked, neither of them said anything. Jim's thoughts were riveted on the word fugitive. It was true. He was a fugitive now,

61

running from the law.

"Do you want to keep your old plates?" Tom asked.

"I'm sorry," Jim replied, "I was thinking about what you said. I am a fugitive."

"That's right my friend. Now do you want to keep your old license plates, or not?"

"I guess I'd better. You know, I still have the license plates from my first car. Or at least they're back at the house."

"Let's go for a walk," Tom suggested. "We shouldn't be talking so close to the road."

"I want to thank you, Tom," Jim said, as they walked the trail that led to lake. "I know you're taking a risk to help me like this. You're a good friend."

"It makes me mad that I have to be doing it, Jim. You're no criminal. Friend or no friend, if I thought you were dangerous, I would be the first one to turn you in. Darn it. You've been a blessing to this community. What you teach is positive. I know that I haven't been much interested in lengthy discussions about our personal beliefs, but I've been watching you and seeing the effect that your work has had in the lives of others. Do you know what first impressed me about you? When you coached Little League baseball, you were more concerned about your kids than about winning. Everybody played on your team. I remember when you started little Timmy White. He was the happiest kid on the ball field that day. Your Jesus isn't just a Jesus of words."

"Tom, my greatest joy would be that, instead of saying 'your Jesus,' you would be able to say 'my Jesus.'"

"To do so now would be costly, my friend."

"Indeed it would. But promise me, Tom, that you'll think about it."

"I have been," Tom replied, surprising Jim.

They walked along for awhile in silence. It was not an uncomfortable silence, as often exists when two people search in vain for something relevant or clever to say. It was a comfortable silence, where Tom and Jim were allowed to explore their thoughts.

As they arrived at the lake, Jim broke the silence. "Why do they only want to arrest me?"

"It's not only you. They've already arrested Pastor Samuels. I understand. I'm not sure why the other pastors are not being sought as well."

"But why only the pastors? Aren't the members of our congregations breaking the very same law?"

"Yes," explained Tom. "But Wisconsin has seen what has happened in the other states, the overcrowding of the prison system and the stress on the budget. For now, it has been decided to go after the leaders only. They hope that arresting you will silence the rest. Sam Johansen and others are pressuring for your lay leaders to be arrested as well. There's something else I have to tell you, Jim. The papers and newscasts have spoken some about it, but the truth is that we are much closer to giving over our national sovereignty to the Global Union than what has been reported. It could happen as early as January. If it does take place, the debate over what to do with all the religious extremists will be a mute issue. You will be forced either to deny your faith or be beheaded."

"Well, I guess I won't be the first to have it happen, nor the best."

"You'll be one of the best. I won't speak to you about changing your beliefs," Tom continued. "If the truth be known, I respect them and your willingness to be true to them even if it means your death. I'd think less of you if you were to betray your conscience now. But you don't have to be stupid. Don't run towards your enemies. I've asked you before, and I ask you again, not only for your own sake, but for that of Sandy and the children: Get out of here."

"I promised you that I would, Tom. My car is packed and I'm ready to go."

"Sam Johansen knows you well. He will not rest until you are behind bars. He knows where you're most likely to run to. They know that Sandy and the children have been staying at your father-in-law's farm. They will look for you there."

Darkness was stretching itself out over the lake and the forest. Again the two men stood in silence looking out over the lake. Jim bent down and skipped a stone across its smooth surface. "I'd rather be fishing."

Laying his hand on Jim's shoulder, Tom said, "I'd like to hear the police talking about the fish that got away. Are you ready to go?"

"Not yet," replied Jim. "I'm going to stay here awhile yet. I've got a few things to think out before I head off." Taking Tom's right hand in both of his, Jim, his voice breaking with emotion, repeated, "Thank you again, my friend. If they catch me, come and see me in jail."

Tom embraced Jim in a crushing hug that seemed to last for a long time. Finally, Jim pushed away. "Go, Tom. Your family will be wondering where you are. There's nothing more that you can do for me now. Think about your relationship with God."

"I will," Tom assured him. "And you be careful."

Tom turned and headed back up the trail to his car. Jim watched as he vanished into the darkness. From deep within Jim's spirit welled up the prayer, "Thank you, Lord, for a good friend like Tom. Help him to believe in you. Help him to know that he has more to gain than he has to lose by accepting You as his Lord and Savior, even in these difficult times."

Chapter 9

In truth, Jim really didn't need to think anything through. He had already made his plans, but he wanted a few minutes to be alone with God. His visit with Tom had helped to calm him down. Although the darkness enshrouded him, he was not as jumpy or frightened as he had been when he first drove up Swede's Hill.

Jim was grateful and gave thanks that, for the time being, his fellow believers in Green Bluff would not be imprisoned. It had been a good decision, he felt, that they would now meet clandestinely. They would be able to continue to worship and encourage one another, but the authorities would think that their strategy had worked, and that the arrest order made out in the name of their pastor had been sufficient to disperse and discourage the congregation.

Jim thought of Peter Samuels. Was he okay? Jim laughed to himself. Clearly Pastor Samuels was ready for anything. In their conversations since the shooting of the Supreme Leader, it seemed to Jim that Peter was almost enthusiastic about the possibility of suffering for Christ's sake. And why shouldn't he be? Surely Pastor Samuels' reward would be great in heaven. Jim prayed that he would be strong to face whatever he might be experiencing in that moment.

Jim thought of Sandy and the children. Soon he would be seeing them again and they would join him in a fugitive lifestyle. He prayed for their joint safety and that the Lord would guide their family as clearly as He had guided the Israelites through their wilderness journey. The plan as to what to do when this moment arrived had been worked out together with Sandy and her folks. Jim had wanted to protect the family as much as he could, for as long as he could, but Sandy had been insistent that they would face the situation together. Jim thanked God for a godly and courageous wife.

Jim thought of his fellow believers who at that very moment were suffering and dying throughout the world for their faith in Christ. He prayed that they would be faithful to the end, and that by their testimony, their very persecutors might come to repentance and faith. He thought of his own mortal enemy, Sam Johansen. Sam was so filled with hate. "Lord, soften his heart toward you," Jim prayed. After a short time, Jim made his way back to his car. Tom had left. Jim removed the branches from behind and atop his vehicle. He walked over to where he could see Green Bluff one more time. "Good-bye for now," he said, in an audible voice. He started the car and headed north, in the direction of his in-laws' farm. He felt that his note to Ron would have the police waiting long enough for him to make an easy and safe escape. Forty-five minutes into the journey, he stopped at a crossroads gas station and phoned Sandy. He explained that the arrest order had been made out in his name, and that he was now a fugitive. He would be there in forty-five minutes. She should have the children ready for when he arrived.

Jim was careful to remain within the speed limit. He was passed once by a police car and passed a second one at a crossroads. His heart raced each time, but thankfully they seemed disinterested in him. Jim was glad that Tom had thought to bring him the false plates.

Jim arrived at his in-laws' farm at 9:45. Sandy greeted him with a big hug, which quickly turned into a family affair as Caleb, Ashley, and Carol joined in. They had a special family name for their communal hugs. They called them "munglepucks." Jim could remember no other munglepuck which he appreciated more than the one in which he now participated. After about a minute of munglepucking, hair ruffling, and picking up of the children in his arms, Grandma Peterson, ever the practical one, said, "All right... all right, children. Your father must be hungry. Let's continue this reunion inside."

With all that had happened, Jim had completely forgotten about supper, but when he entered into the Petersons' kitchen and smelled his mother-in-law's beef stew, he realized how hungry he was. "Mom, you shouldn't have, but I'm glad you did." After filling himself with a plate and a half of his mother-in-law's cooking, Jim began to inform the family of what had taken place that day. At first, he had thought of asking the children to leave while he did it, but he changed his mind, knowing that they would need to know the truth. He explained to the children that they had been staying at Grandma and Grandpa's farm, not just because they were on vacation, but because there were bad people who were trying to hurt Christians, and that they had felt that the children would be safer at the farm than in Green Bluff. Jim explained that the bad people wanted to arrest him, and that Daddy had to leave Green Bluff, too, and that they might never be able to go back there.

Carol interrupted, "Daddy, do you mean that you are a criminal?"

"We all are, Carol," Jim addressed her, "but not because we've done anything wrong. People who don't love Jesus have made a law against those of us who do. But right now, they only want to arrest Daddy."

"Well, I don't want those bad people to arrest you!" Carol said, partly in anger and partly in fear, her eyes wide and filling with tears.

Jim reached out and hugged her to himself. "Neither do I, Honey, and that's why I came here to be with you, and that's why you, Caleb, Ashley, your mom, and I are going to go camping for awhile in Grandpa and Grandma's woods. It will be safer for us there than in the house."

Caleb looked pensive. "How long will we have to stay there?"

"I don't know, Caleb," answered Jim.

"I've never camped in the snow before. I could help to get firewood so that we could keep warm."

"Thank you, Caleb," Sandy joined in. "We'll need that."

"Will we have to do school work?" asked Ashley.

"Well, we won't bring any of the school books, but we will learn in other ways," responded Sandy.

"Will Grandpa and Grandma be coming?" asked Carol.

"I wish we could," said Grandpa. "There's nothing I like better than camping. But I'm afraid that somebody has to keep an eye out for the cows. I'll come visit you as often as I can, though."

Satisfied with that answer, Carol went on to her next and probably most important question, "Can I bring Snugly Bear?"

"Oh yes," answered Jim, "Snugly Bear will most certainly have to go with us. Why don't you three go and get anything you think you might want to take along. Don't forget to bring some games. We'll have to leave in about 15 minutes."

With the children gone, Mrs. Peterson served up some coffee and Jim explained to his in-laws what Tom had said about the decision to only arrest church leaders for the time being in Wisconsin and about the possible uniting of the United States with the Global Union. That said, Jim went outside and unloaded everything that he had in the car onto a flatbed trailer, which was attached to his father-in-law's tractor. Mr. and Mrs. Peterson busied themselves loading up food supplies, jugs of water, mattresses, and some bales of hay. Sandy bundled up the children and got them and their things onto the wagon.

Fortunately, it had been a dry fall and the farm roads were easily passable, even in Jim's sedan. Grandma led the way with a flashlight. They didn't want to put on their headlights for fear that a neighbor might see them. Car or tractor headlights in the fields at that time of night would definitely attract attention and comment. Jim followed in his car, and Grandpa brought up the rear, covering over any tracks with the tractor that might be made by the car. Mrs. Peterson led the way to an old dump area where Mr. Peterson used to take his children to do some shooting. It was littered with old bottles, kitchen appliances, a gutted and rusted out Oldsmobile Cutlass, and assorted farm machinery. It was a grown over area, with small sycamore trees dominating. Jim parked the car as near as he could to a stand of sycamores that stood just below an overhanging embankment. Mr. Peterson put on his headlights, and they all worked to cover-up and camouflage the vehicle.

That done, they climbed onto the wagon and Grandma led the way to what would be their new home. The Peterson farm was a large one, land wise. The place where Grandma was leading them was only accessible by farm tractor or a four-wheel drive vehicle. Sandy remembered the woods from her younger days. She had often explored them with her friends and two older brothers. It was a densely forested area of approximately nine acres. From time to time Mr. Peterson would chop down some of the trees for fire wood, but largely it was left alone. One tractor path passed through it, but that too was largely overgrown now.

"One advantage to camping now is the fact that there won't be very many bugs," Sandy commented to Jim and the children.

Grandpa stopped the tractor on the eastern edge of the forest. "Okay," he said, "This is where we get off. Grab a flashlight and whatever you can carry." A footpath led about 200 feet into the woods. It had been well cleared by Mr. Peterson during the previous month, "just in case," and was easily passable, even for the children. At the end of it was a clearing, surrounded on all sides by ash and maple trees and smaller undergrowth. Mr. Peterson was a man of detail. Awaiting them was a circle of six hay bales surrounding a fire pit, complete with a grill. Obviously Mr. Peterson planned on visiting. To one side of the clearing there was enough firewood stacked for probably a month. Seeing Jim's eyes looking in that direction, Mr. Peterson shrugged. "I didn't know how often I'd be able to safely make it back here to see you. I wanted you to be prepared."

"I do have an ax with me, you know," Jim stated. "And there are trees here. What if we never had to use this place?"

"I figured it would be a great place to come camping with the grand kids," Mr. Peterson replied.

When they lit the kerosene lamp, Jim could see even better that Sandy and his father-in-law had chosen their location well. Mr. Peterson laid down a heavy bed of straw on the ground underneath where they set up the tent. Afterwards Jim, Sandy, and Mr. Peterson made many trips bringing down mattresses, sleeping bags, blankets, food, and other supplies. Before they were done, Carol and Ashley had both fallen asleep.

When everything was in order for the night, Mr. and Mrs. Peterson hugged Caleb, Sandy, and Jim, said their good-byes, and headed up the trail to the tractor. At the top of the trail, they paused to cover up the entrance, and then were on their way. Mrs. Peterson went on foot, leading the tractor with her flashlight.

Things, though desperate, had gone well. The only concern that they had now was the possibility of meeting the police on their return to the house and barn. It would be difficult to explain why Mr. Peterson was driving his tractor around in the middle of the night with the lights off.

Chapter 10

Arriving back at the barn, the Petersons breathed a prayer of thanks to God. The police were not waiting for them. After putting the tractor away, they entered the house and retired to bed for a night of fitful sleep.

The police arrived early the next day.

They were polite at first. Mrs. Peterson answered them at the door, as her husband was in the barn milking the cows. "Hello, Mrs. Peterson," said an officer. He was six feet tall, muscular and in his early forties. "I'm Officer Grady," he said, showing her his badge. "This is Officer Highland. I wonder if we might have a few words with you and your husband."

"Of course, Officer Grady," Mrs. Peterson replied. "My husband is in the barn, but I would be glad to answer any of your questions. Won't you come in and have a cup of coffee? I've seen you often in town. You've lived here for four or five years now. Isn't that right? And my goodness, you don't need to introduce Officer Highland to me. He dated my Sandy a couple of times, if I remember right. It's good to see you again, Joe."

"Thank you, Mrs. Peterson," continued Officer Grady, a bit uncomfortable at being the one questioned. "We are here on business. We understand that your daughter Sandy and her children have been living with you for the last couple of months."

"Why, yes she has," said Mrs. Peterson disarmingly. "Word spreads fast in a small community. But I'm afraid you've missed her. She and the children left late last night with her husband Jim."

"Is that a fact? You see Mrs. Peterson, we received a call at the station from the police in Green Bluff. It seems as if your son-in-law is a fugitive. An order was issued for his arrest there yesterday. They rightly guessed that he would flee here to be with his family."

"A fugitive? Pray tell," began Mrs. Peterson her anger building. "What terrible crime did he commit? Did he rob a bank? Did he

71

shoot someone down in cold blood? Did he run over someone with his car while driving drunk? Did he kidnap a child? Or is it that, oh no, not that. Please don't tell me that he's one of those Christians. They're so dangerous and unpredictable."

Noting the sarcasm in her voice, Joe Highland attempted to diffuse the situation. "Please, Mrs. Peterson, we don't make the laws. We're just doing our job, however unpleasant it may be at times."

"Joe," Mrs. Peterson said hotly, "you should be ashamed of yourself and you know it." She paused to reign in her anger. After an awkward moment of silence, she continued. "I'm sorry gentlemen. No I'm not. I'm not sorry at all. Jim and Sandy are not here. They left the house hurriedly last night in their car, no doubt expecting such a visit from you. You are welcome to search the place for them, but only if you would be so kind as to show me a search warrant. We don't want you to be disappointed, however, and show up empty handed to your superiors. I, gentlemen, am a Christian, as is my husband. You may arrest us. We believe that Jesus Christ was and is God, and that faith in Him is the only hope that we have in this life or the next. Consider it, gentlemen. Is doing your job pay enough for eternal suffering in hell?"

"Mrs. Peterson," interrupted Officer Grady. "We did not come here for a sermon, though a very fine one it was. Nor do we have an arrest order for you or your husband. When we do, you may be sure that we will fulfill our duty. You, Mrs. Peterson, should consider your allegiance to the United States Government, instead of to some God you can neither see nor touch. If you see or hear from your daughter or her husband, we would appreciate it if you would call us. Good day." With that, the officers returned to their car and drove off.

Things were relatively quiet at the Peterson farm during the next couple of weeks. Officer Grady, accompanied by a police officer from Green Bluff, showed up two days after his first visit, this time with a search warrant. What they found confirmed what Mrs. Peterson had said to him two days earlier. For all appearances, Sandy and the children had left the house hurriedly, presumably with Jim and on the night that Jim's arrest order was given. The children's school books, along with clothes and toys had been left behind in their escape. They could be anywhere by now. The Petersons' registered vehicles were still there at the farm, so presumably they had fled in Jim's car.

Mr. Peterson waited for four days before he took the manure spreader out towards the camp site. There he found a happy family, enjoying one another's company as they had not been able to do for the previous two months. There, in their protected hideout, the arrest order and the laws against Christians seemed to be distant problems. Caleb eagerly showed Grandpa a teepee they had built from fallen branches. After unloading the food supplies and extra blankets he had brought and stored in a wooden box under the manure, Jim and Sandy invited him to stay on for lunch. Mr. Peterson declined, saying it was still too early to be gone so long from the house without explanation. He would come again with his wife as soon as they thought it safe. They all walked to the end of the trail together and said their good-byes. Jim and Sandy and the children watched as Grandpa started up the tractor and began to spread the manure on the field.

Meanwhile, the Global Union continued to implement changes with amazing speed and efficiency and extended its field of influence and control throughout the world. Perhaps some of the most important discussions were taking place in the area of religion and economics.

Pope Adrian, together with the leaders of a myriad of religious traditions, had been meeting weekly since the challenge had been placed before them in Prague to formulate a focus of religious faith that, instead of dividing the world's people, would unite them together as one. This was not an easy task. They began by discussing the possibility of choosing one of the existing world religions as the official religion, and forcing those of other traditions to adopt its beliefs and practices. This was quickly discarded. Instead of unifying them, this suggestion tore the group apart and turned what was meant to be discussion and debate into open division and dispute. Some argued that their religion should be adopted because it had the largest number of followers in the world. Others argued that it should be theirs, because their faith had taken root and had established communities in every part of the globe. Others said, no, it should be theirs, for theirs was the most ancient of all faiths. Others said it should be theirs, for theirs is the most recent and therefore the most evolved. Some argued on the basis of their sacred books, and some on the excellence of their earthly leaders. Although all of the leaders were, one might say, apostates, who had some time before ceased to hold fervently to the beliefs of their particular faiths, they were none the less quite attached to the forms and ceremony thereof and quite unwilling to give them up.

Were it not for the extraordinary skills of Pope Adrian and the political pressure of the Global Union, the issue would have deadlocked and ended there. Instead, Pope Adrian asked that a massive tapestry be lifted before all of those present. At first, he showed the back side of the tapestry. It seemed a disorganized jumble of threads, knots, and colors. "This is how we are today. This is how we have been for centuries and millenniums: contrasting and clashing. As this tapestry is a mess, so our world has been a disorganized and ugly mess. But that does not mean that each of these colors and threads are not important. They are." Speaking to those who had lifted the tapestry, he said, "Please turn the tapestry." There before them was perhaps the most beautiful tapestry any of them had ever seen. "This is how we must be. Our religions and traditions are important. They must not be eliminated in favor of only one. If we remove all the colors except one, the tapestry of our life would be very dull. We must appreciate one another's traditions, but we must find a unifying theme which brings our traditions and practices together as a beautiful picture instead of a disorganized mess."

Option two was to seek common links shared by all of the religious beliefs and traditions, and build a unifying faith system on the basis of these. Although they found themes that were common to many, such as blood, sacrifices, holy places, an afterlife, personal experiences with "God," and the doing of good works, the definitions and specifics about these matters were so diverse among the religions, that it was impossible to come to any sort of consensus. As they struggled with these matters, the theologians and holy men and women of the various traditions became aware of just how false the statement was that said, "All religions are basically the same."

The third option, and the one which seemed the best and only workable solution, was to look outside of the existing religions to build a unifying faith allegiance and cultic practice around someone or something else. They took their example for this from ancient Rome. The people of ancient Rome enjoyed freedom to worship many and various gods, and to do so in the way they thought best. But over and above these lesser gods and religious practices, the people had to swear allegiance to Caesar as the Supreme Deity. Emperor worship was the religious glue that unified the empire. Those who refused to acknowledge the deity of Caesar and swear primary allegiance to him were viewed as subversives and traitors and were killed in various and sundry ways.

All agreed that this was the answer. In this way, religious freedom and diversity could be maintained and practiced, thus guaranteeing the continuance of all of the colors in the tapestry. At the same time, there would be an overarching spiritual and religious focus which would be shared by all. The Supreme Leader, who already enjoyed the confidence and adoration of the majority of the world's people, was the obvious choice around whom this new religion must be formed. Along with his title, Supreme Leader, he would be declared to be God, the Most High. Great statues would be made in his likeness to be adored in public events. Each relational unit would be required to place an image of God, the Most High, in a prominent place in their home. Hymns would be written for the purpose of his worship. Holidays and rituals would be devised or adapted to focus upon his person.

The religious leaders discussed the best time and place for the announcement of the Supreme Leader's deity. After much debate, Jerusalem's Temple Mount, being the geographical focal point of three of the world's largest religions, was chosen. There would be media build up of the event several weeks before. "Let us, the world, go up to Jerusalem and worship our God," was chosen as the motto. Religious events would begin the Sunday prior to Palm Sunday. The Supreme Leader would visit many of the holy places of the world's largest religions during the first week, being identified with and exalted above the founders of these faiths. Then, on Palm Sunday, he would enter Jerusalem on a donkey to the adoration of thousands. On Good Friday, the story of the Supreme Leader's life would be replayed throughout the world. Special emphasis would be placed on the assassination attempt which occurred in Prague and the fact that, in spite of such hateful opposition, the Supreme Leader had chosen to continue in public service, "giving his life" for "his people." On Calvary's Mount, he would be declared to be the savior of the world. The culmination would occur on Easter Sunday morning. The Supreme Leader would enter the Holy of Holies in the Jewish Temple, sit upon the Mercy Seat, and proclaim himself to be, "God, the Most High." A great statue would be unveiled and sacrifices would be presented to him by the various religious leaders of the world. They would then corporately bow down before him and worship him as God.

There were many details to be worked out, but all agreed that the idea was a sound one. Many worried that some of their followers, who held to more literal/fundamental views of their religion, would rebel against such emperor worship. The biggest obstacle they foresaw, however, and one to which they had no answer, was how to insure that every Global Union citizen would so worship the Supreme Leader, exalting him above everything else which they had previously called God.

Meanwhile, the economic ministers of the Global Union, with the many new countries which were being absorbed into the Union, were working hard to keep up with the problem of currencies. Over the years, first with checking accounts, then credit cards, then direct withdrawals from the bank, then electronic transactions by way of the Internet and the global web, the use of hard currency in economic matters had diminished greatly. The nations, however, had never found a way to eliminate entirely the custom of buying and selling with hard currency. Added to this, of course, was the problem of the multitude of independent banks, credit cards, etc. The Supreme Leader not only demanded of his economic ministers a unified currency, which might have been easily achieved by forcing all the joining nations to change to the Euro, but he also demanded a better system of control and accountability.

Their answer to his demand was drastic. All currencies would be eliminated, along with credit cards, checking accounts and banks. In their place, would stand a centralized computer bank listing the wealth and economic resources of each individual. The wealth, stored in individual accounts would be accessed for the varied purposes of buying, selling and taxation, through computer chips installed in the body of each citizen. Corporations and businesses would be issued credit cards, whose access would be limited to individuals approved by the businesses to carry out transactions in their name. Scanners, which would be directly connected to the central data bank, would be installed in all businesses. For example, if a person wanted to buy two pounds of bananas at the local supermarket, he would pass his hand over the supermarket's scanner. There before the cashier would appear a green or a red light. Green would mean that the shopper had sufficient funds to buy the bananas. Red would mean that he did not. In the event of a green light, an automatic transaction would occur whereby the price of the bananas would be withdrawn from the shopper's account and deposited immediately into the supermarket's account. The shopper, in turn, would receive a receipt detailing the beginning balance of his account, the price of the item purchased, and the closing balance of his account. In the event that items should be returned, the process would be reversed. For those shoppers who desired to do their purchasing through the global web, home scanners would be made available to be used in conjunction with a personal password. The ministers proposed that the choice be given to the citizens of the Global Union as to the placement in their bodies of the computer chip. Due to their easy and universal accessibility, the ministers suggested the forehead and the right hand as two possible options.

The technology for such a centralized, computer chip based economy had been in place for many years. Chips had been used on a limited basis by various nations for the controlling of immigrants and the avoiding of fraud on the part of those receiving government social payments. Economists and technicians had discussed the theory of such a cashless society since the onset of the computer chip. The idea made sense, but the conditions had never been right to implement it before. The ministers now believed that the conditions were as ideal as they ever would be for such a drastic shift to a cashless society. They proposed a year's time for the transition to fully be applied.

The reports from Pope Adrian and the economic ministers of the Global Union arrived on the desk of the Supreme Leader within two days of one another. The Supreme Leader was in agreement with both proposals and immediately saw the connection between them. The citizens of the Global Union would worship him as their supreme deity or they would not eat. The implantation of the computer chip would be dependent upon a prior declaration of faith and act of worship directed towards himself as "Most High God." Those who refused to worship him out of higher allegiance to another deity would not be able to receive the chip, and thus would be denied the rights of buying and selling.

On the first of November, the Supreme Leader contacted Pope Adrian and his economic ministers, approving their plans and urging them to go ahead at full speed. In fact, he demanded of his economic leaders that they go ahead at greater than full speed. The first chips were to be installed the following Easter, as a public reward to those who would first bow and adore him in Jerusalem. Theirs would be the example that all would have to follow in the subsequent 90 day period, at the end of which time, all currencies, checks, and credit cards would be of no economic value. Realizing the immensity of the educational and technological aspects of the task being given them, the Supreme Leader made the economic transition the number one priority of his administration and placed almost unlimited financial and people resources at the disposal of the economic task force charged with overseeing the transition.

The reaction was somber when word of the Global Union's decision to move rapidly to a cashless society reached the leaders of the nations that had maintained their independence from the Union. Most depended heavily upon trading with the Union to maintain their economic prosperity and standard of living. Word was that such trading would cease to be possible as soon as plans for the cashless economy were implemented within the Global Union. The United States, Russia, China, Japan, the Muslim nations, Switzerland and a handful of other independent states would be forced to either join the Union, to be self sufficient, or to strengthen economic and trading ties with one another.

Chapter 11

No one on the town council believed it would do any good to try and convince Peter Samuels to renounce his faith, but they knew that they must at least feign an effort. The minister of the United Church readily volunteered for the task, eager to show his errant brother his theological errors. After three visits to the jail, he reported back to the council that Samuels' case was a hopeless one. Tom Watson suggested that someone on the town council attempt to warn Peter away from his stubborn position on the authority of the Bible. In perhaps the best acting job of his life, he insisted, "He has a wife and kids. Doesn't he know the seriousness of this? He could spend the rest of his days in jail or worse if he continues this course." As no one else on the council seemed interested in the task, Tom reluctantly relented to be the man who would meet with Rev. Samuels. Inwardly, he rejoiced at having a perfect excuse to go and have some of his questions answered.

Arriving at the jail on the morning of November third, Tom asked the guards for a room where he and prisoner Samuels could be alone and uninterrupted in their conversation. He was led to one of the visiting rooms where he awaited Rev. Samuels' arrival. The room was sparsely furnished. There were two chairs facing one another from opposite sides of a rectangular table. There was only one door, the one through which he had entered. In the upper third of the door was a small window through which the guards would frequently peer to make sure everything was all right. Tom was glad to see that there were no mirrors. He walked around the room a few times, looking to see if there might be any listening devises present. When he was satisfied that there were not, he sat down and waited. He felt a little ridiculous for his suspicions and caution, but after all, he was entering into dangerous territory.

After several minutes, a guard opened the door and led in a handcuffed Peter Samuels. "If you have any problems, Mr. Watson, just yell. We'll be close by."

"Thank you," responded Tom, "but I don't think that will be necessary."

Reverend Samuels was dressed in a loose orange prison jumper. He was well groomed, and looked Tom right in the eyes. Tom observed that he was not the broken man that he had expected to see. In spite of his present circumstances, Reverend Samuels carried himself with dignity and confidence.

"Please sit down Rev. Samuels," Tom encouraged.

"Thank you, Mr. Watson. Please call me Peter. I remember meeting you briefly several times in the past."

"Yes, that's right, and under more pleasant circumstances."

"This may be hard for you to believe, Mr. Watson, but my circumstances are not as bad as they might seem on the surface. In fact, I have never felt more alive than I do right now. The food's not bad. I've slept in more uncomfortable beds. I have so many people wanting to see me that the authorities are turning them away. But most of all, I finally know."

"You finally know?" asked Tom, unable to hold back his curiosity.

"Yes, I finally know," repeated Peter. "You will know, Mr. Watson, that during our lifetime, being a Christian has been a rather comfortable proposal. As a minister of the Gospel, I've enjoyed the general respect of those in the community, and I've been looked up to by many as an admired teacher and counselor. It may be difficult for you to understand this, but I have always had a nagging doubt about my faith. I sincerely love Jesus, and I have no doubt of His presence and faithfulness in my life. What I haven't known is if I would be faithful to Him if faithfulness became costly. Would my faith be strong enough to withstand persecution, or would I deny my Lord in the moment of difficulty? Now I know. Jesus is my Savior and my Lord. I will willingly go to my death for Him. I know now that I will never be dissuaded from following Him; never. I'm afraid, Mr. Watson, that your mission here this day is in vain."

"My mission this day holds other purposes than you imagine, Rev. Samuels. I'm a friend of Jim Allen. The reason that he is not here with you in jail is that, on the day that your arrest orders were issued, I warned him, and he fled to be with his family. I'm not in agreement with the law which you are accused of breaking. On the day that we parted, I promised Jim that I would consider the claims of Jesus Christ on my life. In fact, I've been unable to escape considering them. They are the final thoughts that I have as I go to sleep, and they are my first thoughts upon awakening in the morning. I haven't been able to escape the issue even in my dreams. I don't know if you are very familiar with the political world, Rev. Samuels. Its two pillars are expediency and compromise. Following your Jesus is not very expedient right now. But I have been increasingly confronted by the consideration of truth. What is true? I know what is not true. The evolutionary theory of the origin of life and species is not true. I have known many people, Rev. Samuels, and the theory that mankind in his core nature is good is not true. Given the right opportunity, most individuals would opt for what is wicked. If they felt that no one would ever know, most people would lie, steal, rape, avenge themselves, and even kill. They tell me now that good and evil do not really exist. They are relative. This too is a lie. Another frequently stated falsehood, Rev. Samuels, is that all religions are basically the same. Most religions, though they speak of an Almighty God, declare that the answers to life are to be found in the efforts of man and in the fulfilling of certain humanly established rituals. Many of your fellow Christian leaders teach the same concept. But, as you will already know, the Bible teaches something very different. The Bible teaches that our greatest needs can only be solved on the basis of what God did and is willing to do. The issue that I'm struggling with right now, Rev. Samuels, is this: If God is the answer to man's needs and problems, why is it that you who have turned to Him are the ones who are suffering the most?"

"If you've been sent to steer me away from my faith, Mr. Watson, you're certainly more subtle about it than Rev. Ebner was. If what you are telling me is true, then you are very close to becoming one of my cell mates. To give you a personal answer to your question," testified Peter, "I am not suffering. For the present I've been denied my liberty to move about as I please. It is very possible, if not probable, that I will be beheaded for my faith in Jesus. Circumstances do not, however, dictate one's misery or joy. That is an internal matter, and it is there that my God abundantly meets my needs. The question, 'Why do bad things happen to good people?'

has been debated since the beginning of time, and I'm sure that many have given better answers than I can give you. The only truly good man to walk this earth suffered greater indignities than I have suffered up to this point in my life. If He died for me, I feel it no great thing that He should ask me to do the same for Him."

"You would have me give my life to Christ and be imprisoned as you have been?"

"I desire, Mr. Watson, that you would know the joy of your sins forgiven. I would have you know the peace of mind which comes from knowing that whether in life or in death that you pertain to the Lord. I would have you know the sure hope of an everlasting inheritance that is far better than you or I can ever begin to imagine. I would have you know the love, the joy, and the peace of walking in the will of God for your life. I would have you do what I believe you know you must do."

"You seem surer of what my convictions are, Reverend Samuels, than I am. We will speak again. Thank you for your time. You've given me a lot to think about."

"You know where I am, Mr. Watson. My time is yours. You do have a Bible?"

"Yes, I do."

"Good. I will ask three requests of you. First, read your Bible. God will guide you to the place where you should start. Second, please call me Peter. Third, if you should have contact with Jim, tell him that I am doing well."

"I will, Rev. Samuels. I mean, Peter."

Tom exited the room, while Peter waited to be escorted back to his cell by the guard.

Peter's time was far from being wasted in jail. Taking up the example of the Apostle Paul, he wrote prison epistles to his congregation, which he was able to send with his wife. She visited every Tuesday and Friday, the only days that Peter was allowed to receive visitors. He made a mental note to ask her to get copies of his letters to the leaders of Green Bluff Baptist Church. Perhaps the letters would be an encouragement to them in this time when their own pastor, Jim, was separated from them.

He already had his next note written:

Dear Friends,

Rejoice with me. The Lord is good. He is giving many opportunities to speak for Him in jail. It will be difficult for the people here to convert to Christ under the present circumstances of threats, but God can do all things. My health is well. I rejoice to see Judy each time she is able to visit me. It would be a great joy if she would be able to come every day. Pray that special permission might be granted for this. I know that many of you have tried to visit me. It is best that instead of trying to visit, you write a note and send it with Judy. I look forward to hearing from you.

Remember the words of Jesus in John 16:33, "In the world you will have tribulation: but be of good cheer; I have overcome the world."

The time is short. Be faithful to Jesus. Soon we will see Him face to face!

Look what I've found in Revelation 2:10: "Fear none of the things which you will suffer: behold, the devil shall cast some of you into prison (THAT'S ME), that you may be tried... be faithful unto death, and I will give you a crown of life."

That's my goal now, to be faithful unto death, however the Lord wills it.

God bless. Be strong.

Your Fellow Servant,

Peter

Little did Peter know that this would be the last letter he would be permitted to send out uncensored. Sam Johansen somehow came into possession of one of the copies. Perhaps it was given to him by a member of the Lutheran Church who had been unaware of his current opposition to the Christian faith. Sam Johansen had become a bitter man. In many ways his life was falling apart. He paid little attention to his business and less attention to his house. Always a well groomed man, he now appeared in public unshaven and disheveled. Word had it that he had begun drinking again; a bad habit which he had left behind after a rebellious period in his late teens and early 20's. His sole focus became the talking down of

Christians. The town council members had become somewhat tired of him, as he seemed to berate one or another of them daily that not enough was being done to stop them. With Peter's letter, he had new ammunition. What good was imprisoning the man if he was allowed to contact his parishioners from his jail cell so freely. Such letters had to stop, or Sam would turn in the whole town council as collaborators with the hated Christians.

The town council decreed that Rev. Samuels would be able to continue receiving mail from his wife on her biweekly visits, but that he would not be permitted to send uncensored mail out. Any letters that he would send out in the future would have to be void of spiritual references.

The members of Green Bluff Baptist Church laid low, meeting, as planned, in a clandestine manner. It was as if Trinity Evangelical Lutheran Church and Green Bluff Baptist Church changed roles. As the members of Green Bluff Baptist Church withdrew into themselves, the normally more reserved believers at Trinity seemed to launch out in public witness as they never had before. The shaking of Jim Allen's theology concerning the rapture of the church had brought about an uncertainty on the part of the believers in his flock. As Jim himself, they were not really certain what they should think or do. In contrast, Rev. Samuels, in the months prior to his arrest, had caught an enthusiasm that he had never had before for Christ and an urgency that he had never demonstrated to proclaim His salvation to the lost. Time was short, he announced. The worldwide persecution of the body of Christ was in full swing. The antichrist was on the scene. Soon he would declare himself to be God. Jesus, in rapturing His Church, would show him different. The unbelieving world would then see the great outpouring of the wrath of God. No matter what it would cost personally, each one had to tell his neighbors and friends, his family and coworkers, that now is the day of salvation. His enthusiasm had been contagious, and his people became bold.

Chapter 12

Back at the farm, what had been a great adventure for the first two weeks, became a trial for the Allen family by the third. The small living and sleeping quarters of the tent gave little opportunity for quiet and personal reflection. The games, which they had so enjoyed together when they first arrived, had become monotonous after playing them for the twentieth time. Jim and Sandy tried to be creative, but their resources were limited. Three days of consecutive rain only worsened the problem.

It was, however, during those three days of rainy weather that Jim remembered and took up Peter Samuels' challenge to read again the scriptures which he thought he had known so well. He began reading in Matthew 24, with Jesus' private words to His disciples. Verses 4 - 6 spoke of the coming of antichrists and wars and rumors of wars. These would happen, as they had happened throughout the centuries, but were not to be taken as signs of the end. Verse 7 indicated an increase in wars, famines, pestilence and earthquakes in diverse places. This had undoubtedly occurred in the months just prior to the formation of the Global Union. The world had suffered widespread catastrophes in those months such as it never had before. The desperate situation in which the world found itself was in large part the reason that it had turned to the then European Union for help and leadership. This was to be taken as a sign of the beginning of the end.

Then Jim's eyes fell upon verses 9-13, "Then shall they deliver you up to be afflicted, and shall kill you: and you shall be hated of all nations for my name's sake. And then shall many be offended, and shall betray one another, and shall hate one another...And because iniquity shall abound, the love of many shall wax cold." Well, he was certainly right in the middle of those verses. He knew that, even as he read, many believers were being killed for their faith in Jesus. In his mind, he could see the faces of those who had turned away from the One whom they had called Savior and Lord. "But he that shall endure to the end, the same shall be saved," verse 13 continued. "O Lord," Jim prayed, "Let me be one of these who endures."

Verse 14 spoke of the condition that the Gospel would be preached in all the world as a witness to all nations; and then the end would come. Jim believed that this prophecy, the completion of the Great Commission, had finally reached its fulfillment in his lifetime. Verse 15, Jim read slowly, spoke of the abomination that causes desolation standing in the holy place. Jim had always understood "the holy place" to refer to the Jewish Temple in Jerusalem and the "abomination of desolation" to refer to the antichrist, or an image of him, being set up in the Temple and being declared to be God. Jim turned back at this point to Daniel 9:25-27, where Daniel also prophesied of the "abomination of desolation." There it spoke of one who would come and who would put an end to sacrifice and offerings, setting up, instead, this "abomination." Jim turned as well to Second Thessalonians 2:1-4. There, Paul wrote to the Thessalonians to encourage them not to be fooled by false proclamations that Jesus had already returned the second time, when He hadn't. Paul assured them, that the day of Christ would not come until there was a falling away from the faith on the part of many believers in Jesus and until the man of sin would be revealed. This man of sin would oppose and exalt himself over all that is called God or that is worshiped. He would sit in God's temple and proclaim himself to be God.

There was no mistaking it. Jim was sure he had a clear biblical picture of the event that these passages pointed to. The problem Jim had was that he had always been taught, had always believed, and had always proclaimed that the church of Jesus Christ would not be on the earth when the antichrist/man of sin/abomination of desolation would so declare himself to be God. Jesus would have come for His Church before that time and raptured it up into heaven with Him. But why had he believed this? He must see it again in God's Word.

He read the Daniel passage again. There was no specific information there regarding any rapture of the church. He reread Matthew 24:1-15. There was no indication given there that a rapture of the church would take place before the antichrist's blasphemous boast. He turned back to Second Thessalonians. He knew what he would find. There it was in verses 6 and 7. The antichrist had been being held back by someone or something. Until that someone or something was taken out of the way, the antichrist could not be revealed. Jim knew his answer to whom that someone was. It was the Holy Spirit residing in the church. The church would have to be raptured (and the Holy Spirit's presence with it) before the man of sin could operate with such boldness and effectiveness. There it was!!! Or was it? Could there be another explanation as to whom this withholding influence could be? Jim looked in vain the rest of the day to find substantiating biblical evidence for the opinion which he had held. The fact was, that although Paul assumed in Second Thessalonians 2:6 that the church knew who this withholding influence was, there was no firm evidence in the Scriptures to definitively identify him or it. The opinion that he had always held still seemed the most logical to him, but, under the circumstances, he wondered whether he had been wrong.

He would continue his study, but it was time for him to try and entertain the kids.

"How about a story?" he suggested to the kids, who were fighting over their turn to play on the battery operated toy computer. "Great," they yelled, and they all got up and ran over and jumped on their dad. Sandy flashed him an appreciative smile, and laid on her back and closed her eyes.

The next time Jim had the opportunity to continue his study was five days later at the Peterson home. It had been over a week since the Petersons had noticed any type of police surveillance. Jim, Sandy and the kids hadn't had a bath in over three weeks. They were tired of the tent. So they decided to take the risk of going to the house. After all, it was only Jim who was in danger of arrest. Jim thought he would almost prefer jail, if only he could take a hot shower and get a decent shave. Clean clothes had not been a problem, as Mr. Peterson had kept them supplied on his manure spreading runs.

Still, they did not want to do anything foolish, so they left the campsite after dark, and walked to the farm house by the light of the three quarter moon. What joy they had in stepping into the Peterson's home. They were greeted by the smell of roasting chicken, and by the hugs and smiles of Grandpa and Grandma Peterson. Ashley and Carol took the first bath, followed by Caleb, Jim, and Sandy. It felt great to be clean again!

The original plan had been to stay through one day and return to the camp site the following night. For many reasons, the arriving winter cold not the least among them, they decided on a different strategy. The Allens would stay at the farm house. During the day, they would stay inside and in the back part of the house...the dining room/kitchen area and the upstairs back bedrooms, where they would be less likely to be seen by people walking or driving by. Duke, the Peterson's 4-year-old German shepherd, who was normally tied on his run, would be given free run of the farm. He had never bitten anyone, but his greeting bark was often misinterpreted by guests as a threat to do so. His bark would serve both as an alarm, warning the Allens and the Petersons of approaching outsiders, and as a means of slowing an outsider's approach to the house. In the event of visitors, the Allens would do a quick pick up of the house and head upstairs, while the Petersons would attempt to greet the guests in the yard. If all else failed, several hiding places were prepared for Jim, as well as an escape plan for him to return to the camping area alone, if necessary. At night the kids would be allowed to go over to the hayloft to burn off some energy.

Sandy began teaching the children again their first day back at the house, converting the room where the girls slept into a school room during the day. Ashley, Carol, and Caleb did not protest, they themselves desiring to have a bit of normalcy and structure in their lives again.

This gave Jim opportunity to return to the Scriptures.

He began where he had begun five days earlier. He read Matthew chapter 24, through verse 15. This time he had a notebook and pencil and began to jot down notes. Recalling his conclusions of five days before, he jotted down:

Matthew 24:1-15 **Theme:** The signs of the second coming of Jesus and the end of the age.

First Sign: A drastic increase in wars, famines, pestilence, and earthquakes in divers places. (COMPLETED)

Second Sign: A world wide persecution of the church of Jesus Christ, including martyrdom. (HAPPENING NOW)

Third Sign: The falling away of many believers, even to the point of betraying those whom they had earlier called brothers. (HAPPENING NOW)

Fourth Sign: False prophets shall arise and deceive many. (MANY FALSE PROPHETS NOW, BUT PERHAPS NOT ON ANY GREATER SCALE THAN AT OTHER TIMES)

Fifth Sign: The Gospel will be preached in all the world as a testimony to all nations. (COMPLETED)

Sixth Sign: The abomination of desolation (man of sin: Second Thessalonians 2:3,4) will sit in the temple in Jerusalem and declare himself to be God and will demand to be worshiped. (TEMPLE HAS BEEN RECONSTRUCTED, BUT THIS EVENT IS YET TO TAKE PLACE)

*** There is no indication in Matthew 24 of a rapture taking place prior to the first through the sixth sign. The church must be present for the second and fifth signs. There is also no indication in Daniel of such an event. Second Thessalonians 2:5-8 would indicate a rapture prior to the sixth sign, if it refers there to the Holy Spirit and the Church. But does it?

Jim continued his reading with verse 16 of Matthew 24. What a frightening passage it was. After the abomination of desolation, there would be great tribulation, greater than any experienced from the beginning of the world until that time. Where would God's people be during this great time of tribulation? Verse 22 gave a ray of hope, saying that for the elect those days would be shortened, but in order for them to be shortened, they would have to be present during a part of them. Verse 24 indicated that this would be true as well.

What type of tribulation would it be? Matthew gave no details. What he did say was that at the end of those days of great tribulation, the sun would be darkened and all the powers of the heavens would be shaken. After that, and Jim could hardly believe his eyes, would come the rapture. The rapture would occur sometime after the antichrist's blasphemous claim to be God! As if reading the passage for the first time, Jim stared and stared at verses 30 and 31. How was it possible that he had not seen this before? Jesus could not have used clearer or simpler language. The abomination of desolation would appear, there would be a great time of tribulation, the heavens would go nuts, and Jesus, to the great distress of those who had not believed in Him, would appear in the heavens and gather His church unto himself out of the midst of the suffering. That's the way it would be! Jim couldn't believe it. How could he, a student and teacher of the Bible for so many years, have misunderstood what was so clearly stated by the Master? There had to be other passages which laid out the events in a different order, shedding greater light on what Matthew recorded.

Forgetting his notes, Jim turned to the other gospels. Mark had the same order of events!

What did Luke say? He said the same thing!

First Thessalonians 4:13-5:11 gave no specific information on how the events of rapture would occur, except to say this: When Jesus did return to catch up the church together with Himself in the clouds, those who had died in Christ would rise first, followed directly by the living saints. Jim wasn't interested in the mental gymnastics as to what this meant exactly. He believed it to mean that the bodies of the dead saints would be resurrected to be united with their souls and spirits, which had preceded their bodies to be in the Lord's presence at the moment of their death. He would remain satisfied with the answer for now, as it was the timing of the rapture that was the important matter to him for the moment. He did stop to reflect, however, on how great God's power is to pull something like that off. There is no one like Him!

First Thessalonians also stated that the ungodly would be caught by surprise by the day of the Lord (was this the same as the rapture?), but that the Lord's people would not be surprised by it. It would come like a thief in the night to those who did not believe God's Word, but to those who trust in it, its occurrence and perhaps its timing should not be a surprise. If the "day of the Lord" were synonymous with the rapture, and if chapter 5, verse 4, speaks of the timing of the rapture as well as the occurrence, then the Lord's people would not be surprised when it came because of the fact that very specific events (those mentioned in the gospels) would precede it. If the rapture could have occurred at any time, as Jim had always believed, without preceding events, then how could the godly know of the general timing of its coming any more than the ungodly?

Second Thessalonians, as Jim had read days earlier, affirmed, with the gospels, that the man of sin would declare himself to be God in the temple and demand to be worshiped prior to the rapture.

Jim looked up Second Peter 3. There Peter affirmed that the Lord's promises were sure and He would complete them. Jim felt a bit of shame at reading verse 9. He had begun to doubt God's Word, because, in the way that he had interpreted it, it did not match up with the reality he was living. Never! It was not God who was wrong or unreliable about the rapture, it was he who had been wrong. He breathed a prayer of repentance, asking for God's forgiveness for his doubt. The day of the Lord, in Peter, seemed to refer to the final judgment and utter destruction of the earth, not the rapture. He, too, said it would come as a "thief in the night," not distinguishing between believers and unbelievers. Peter's focus did not seem to be of the timing and the events of the end time, but rather the moral implications that the reality of a final judgment should have on our lives.

That left Revelation. Jim took a break to wrestle on the floor with his children, who had finished with their morning session of school. Sandy asked how his study was going. Jim answered that it was going very well, but that there were a few passages that he had to look at before he came to any final conclusions. Sandy noticed, however, that something had changed about Jim's countenance. It was difficult to pinpoint, but somehow he seemed more joyful and confident than he had been for many months.

After lunch and a lengthy nap, Jim opened his Bible to the book of Revelation. He read from the beginning. The pertinent part to his current study began in chapter 6, when the Lamb, Jesus, began opening the seals:

Seal 1: The rider of the white horse and he that had a bow but no arrow, which Jim understood to mean one who would conquer peacefully. The European Union and the Supreme Leader had indeed done that. They did not need to go to war, as the nations voluntarily yielded their sovereignty over to them.

Seals 2, 3, and 4: The rider of the red horse who had the great sword, who would take peace from the earth and kill many in war; the rider of the black horse with the balance in his hand, who signified famine; and the rider of the pale horse whose name was Death. These three horses coincided with the words of Jesus in the gospels, as to the beginning

of sorrows. Jim flipped back to Matthew 24:7. Listed there were the horses and the riders, who had caused so much havoc in the world.
Seal 5: Slain saints of God, who were martyred for their allegiance to the Word of God and their testimony of faith in the Lord Jesus Christ. The book of Revelation, as well, gave testimony that after the beginning of the tribulation period the saints would be present and greatly persecuted. Was it fear of such persecution that had prevented Jim from seeing the harmony of the biblical passages and the clarity with which they presented the end times events?
Seal 6: Bypassing, for the moment, the mention of the abomination of desolation, the sixth seal would be a great earthquake and heavenly calamity which would cause all men to flee for the mountains and caves to escape from the wrath of the Lamb. It was immediately after such heavenly disorder that the gospels said that Jesus would appear in heaven and gather his elect unto himself, causing those who remained great despair. While not mentioning the actual event of the rapture, John was given a vision of heaven. He saw worshiping before the throne of God and before the Lamb a great multitude from all the nations, clothed in white robes and holding palm branches in their hands. Wondering at who this multitude was, an angel gave John to understand that they were "those which came out of the great tribulation, and have washed their robes, and made them white in the blood of the Lamb." Verses 15-17 indicated that prior to their presence before the throne of God, that they would have suffered hunger and thirst, exposure to the sun, and sorrows causing them tears.

Of course, Jim didn't want to have to go through that! He didn't want to be martyred, and wanted even less to pass through hunger and thirst, heat exposure and great sorrow. No wonder he wanted the rapture to occur before the tribulation started. But he could no longer deny it. He was living in the midst of the tribulation, somewhere between the fifth and sixth seals; somewhere between Matthew 24:14 and Matthew 24:15. As a Christian, what lay before him was either death or the life of a fugitive until the day of the rapture. What had filled him with enthusiasm that morning now filled him with fear. Right now it was he who was on the run. Soon it would be his whole family. Jesus would return. The rapture would occur. But it would not occur before they had suffered in much greater ways than they had already suffered. How much suffering would they have to endure? How much suffering could they withstand?

Jim didn't feel much like turning there, but he knew that he must. Revelation also spoke specifically about the man of sin, or in Revelation, "the beast." Jim turned to chapter 13. Beginning with chapter 10, Revelation turned somewhat from the events of the end times to the personalities thereof. Chapter 13 focused its attention on the two beasts, political and religious, which would work together in opposing God. Jim no longer searched for loopholes, nor for the ways he had tried to interpret the passage in the past. He read in verse 3 about the wound that the first beast would receive, a deadly wound to the head, but a wound that was healed. He read in verse 5 of the great power that was given him for 42 months. He read in verse 6 of how he would blaspheme against God. He read in verse 7 how the beast would make war with the saints throughout the world to try to overcome them. He read in verse 8 about how all upon the earth who were not the Lord's would worship him. He read in verse 10 that the saints would have to have patience and faith for they would be led into captivity and death. He read in verses 11- 15 of a second, miracle producing beast, who would inspire the earth to worship and make images of the first beast. He read in verses 16 - 18 about how all people would be required to receive a mark representing the first beast in their right hand or in their forehead. Without such a mark no one would be permitted to buy or sell. No wonder believers would suffer hunger and thirst.

Jim closed his Bible, stunned by what he had read.

Chapter 13

After the children had gone to bed that evening, Jim sat down with Sandy and his in-laws to discuss the conclusions that he had reached from his reading of the end time passages. They, too, had shared Jim's earlier convictions that the rapture of the church would occur prior to any tribulation period. They listened with interest as Jim led them through one passage of Scripture and then another. Had the circumstances been different, there would have been a lively debate regarding several of the passages, and the introduction of other passages to be considered. As it was, Sandy and the Petersons found themselves nodding in agreement with everything that Jim had to say.

When Jim reached the end of his presentation, Mr. Peterson spoke. "Jim, I've taken a much keener interest in the news than I used to. I've printed up most of the recent articles that have had to do with the Global Union and the Supreme Leader. You're welcome to read through them all, but there's one that I think is of particular interest to what you have said tonight." Mr. Peterson reached over to his filing cabinet and pulled out a thick folder. "Here it is," he said, removing one of the sheets closest to the top. The article was dated November 2nd: "The Global Union will move to a cashless society by April of next year. Currencies, credit cards, checks, and banks will become obsolete under the current plan of the economic ministers of the Global Union and with the support and urging of the Supreme Leader. The bold proposal presented yesterday in Brussels will centralize the financial information of all its citizens, as well as business entities, in one computer bank. Financial transactions will take place directly through a computer chip inserted in the forehead or the right hand of each citizen. The decision by the GU economic ministers places pressure on those nations, such as the United States, which yet remain outside of the Union, as they will become economically isolated from their largest trading partner in the moment that this plan is implemented."

"That gives the United States one more reason to yield over its sovereignty to the Global Union," Jim commented. "It will be impossible for us to stay out now."

"Jim, there is no doubt that what you have said tonight is true," Mr. Peterson continued. "The abomination of desolation is close at hand. We, too, will soon have arrest orders issued in our name, only the threat will not be of imprisonment but of sure death. The rapture will come, but we probably will not live to see it. If we do, it will be through great sufferings. The only other option is to deny Jesus, and that for me is no option."

"Do you think we should talk to the congregation about this?" Sandy asked, turning towards Jim. "They should know about this."

"Yes, I think we should. I've taught them badly enough regarding the rapture. I ought to show them now what the Bible really says. I need to talk to Sven Svensen and Steve Brown," agreed Jim. "Do you think you could go into town tomorrow, Dad, and give them a call, and ask them to meet us here? I don't think anybody would follow them."

"All right, but I want to invite a couple of our elders here as well. You know, our pastor is in jail as well."

"Make sure you can trust them," cautioned Jim.

"It's going to be hard to know who to trust and who not to trust from here on in," reminded Mr. Peterson. "Who would have ever thought that Sam Johansen would have turned out to be your greatest enemy?"

Sven Svensen and Steve Brown arrived two afternoons later, on November 9. Sven parked his car in the barn, where Mr. Peterson normally kept his tractor. There it would be out of sight and less likely to attract attention.

It was all that Jim could do not to run out and meet them in the yard. How glad Jim was to see them. Through the joys and struggles of church leadership, a great bond had formed among their families. Sven and Steve had taken the liberty of bringing their wives along. Actually, they said later, when their wives learned that they were going to see Jim and Sandy, they insisted on going along too. When Jim saw what it meant to Sandy to have them there, he felt foolish and selfish not to have thought to invite them himself.

When they passed through the doors of the entry way, Jim and Sandy were there to meet them with crushing embraces. Jim and Sandy were surprised as tears began to stream down their faces. They had not been aware how great the strain had been on them in the previous months. Seeing their friends triggered an explosion of bottled up emotion that they weren't even aware they had been suppressing. After 10 minutes or so of tears, hugs, and "It's so great to see you," Mrs. Peterson insisted that they move into the dining room. Offers of refreshments by Mrs. Peterson went largely ignored as the three couples caught up on one another's lives, and as Jim and Sandy asked after the various members of the congregation. Ellen Johansen was living temporarily in the parsonage, with her two teen aged children. The core group of believers was continuing faithful. Peter Olsen continued to be the spark plug and encourager of the group.

Sven had brought with him the final letter that Pastor Samuels had been able to send out from the prison. Jim read it aloud to the group. He couldn't believe it! Just reading the letter, Jim knew that Peter was happier suffering for Jesus in the Green Bluff jail then he had ever been in the years that he had known him. Maybe I shouldn't have run, Jim wondered to himself.

The two elders from the Peterson's church, John Dunn and Malcolm Ivy, arrived an hour after the Svensens and the Browns. After introductions, they all moved into the dining room. When they were all seated, Mrs. Peterson was the first to speak. "I didn't make these refreshments to go to waste." At her urging and to her satisfaction, they were finally willing to have some coffee and punch and the cake which she had made for the occasion.

As they ate, Jim took the group through the Scriptures which had convinced him to change his stance on the events of the end times and, particularly, the rapture. He spent much time, as he did so, detailing the events through which they had all lived in the previous few years. Mr. Peterson concluded by reading some of the most recent and most pertinent articles regarding the GU and the Supreme Leader.

"Well, that explains life as it is," commented Sven, after an uncomfortable silence.

"Then what we've believed all along has just been wishful thinking?" asked John Dunn, not wanting to believe it.

"I'm afraid so," said Jim.

"But how can God allow His children to go through such suffering?" John continued. John often did his thinking with his mouth open.

"That's a hard question," answered Jim. "We know that we are not the first of His children to know such hardship. The apostles, almost to a man, were martyred for their faith and testimony. The early believers were thrown by the Roman authorities to the lions and were used as human torches in their gardens. Throughout the history of the church our brothers and sisters in Christ have been imprisoned, tortured, and murdered in the most horrible of ways. We've all read Hebrews 11:36, 37. Jesus Himself was flogged, beaten, spit upon, mocked, and crucified for us. Jesus almost assured us that we would suffer for Him. Only we used to think that that meant getting a cold or having someone laugh at us when we tried to witness to them."

"What is the advantage, than, of being a Christian?" John Dunn pressed on.

"Well," said Margaret Svensen, entering the conversation, "the same as always: The forgiveness of our sins; being accepted as a child of God; having the sure hope of everlasting life in the glorious presence of God; peace and joy in the midst of difficulties and sufferings...I could go on."

"As could I," responded John. "I'm just thinking out loud. Don't take me wrong."

"John, I have asked myself the same questions over and over again the past few months," confessed Jim. "I guess I've reached the point now, though, that I feel these questions to be academic. Suffering is here and now, and I've become convinced by the Scriptures and current events that it is only going to get worse. What I'm not sure of is how to react to it. Should I run and hide, as I have done up to this point, or should I boldly confess my faith in Christ and receive the consequences of it? I'm concerned that I mentally and spiritually prepare myself, and as I am able, the church, so that we will not deny our Lord. What keeps coming to my mind is the teaching of Jesus about the ten virgins, and how five of them did not have sufficient oil in their lamps to be ready to greet the bridegroom when he came."

"Our pastor is in prison," commented Malcolm Ivy, "but he is assured that it will only be temporary. He remains convinced that we are not in the tribulation period, believing, as I believe we all felt, that the rapture would occur before that time. He believes that the governments will realize that what they are doing in terms of the persecution of Christians is wrong. He believes that they will soon reverse themselves to allow freedom of religious belief and expression once again. He's asking us to pray for this and to use whatever influence we have to this end."

"Do you believe that will be effective?" asked Mr. Peterson.

"No," Malcolm had to admit, "I respect him as our pastor, but I think he is wrong in this. I think we are in the midst of the tribulation period and that our prayers ought to be directed toward strength and faithfulness on our part as believers, so as not to deny our Lord. Instead of writing letters to our congressmen and women, we ought to be encouraging one another, as the early church did, to expect, to endure, and to rejoice in the tribulations and suffering which are to come."

"Do you think we should go against what our pastor is teaching?" John asked him.

"If we are agreed on this, we must first try to convince him by the Scriptures as to what we have talked about today. Jim, would you be willing to put down in writing what you've said today? We could go and talk to Pastor Irving, presenting him with the information we've talked about here, and hope that he will agree with us. It will be better to work with him on this rather than against him. But if I know Pastor Irving, such a change in his beliefs about the end times will be difficult."

"If you think they'll help," agreed Jim, "I'll write down my thoughts, and try to have them ready as soon as I can. Right now, though, I need your help in answering the question that I asked before. If we're right, and I think we are, how should we be living now? Should we be preparing hiding places in the wilderness and stockpiling food, running away from our persecutors, or should we be running to them with the Gospel message, that some of them might be saved?"

Mrs. Peterson, who had spent most of her time in the kitchen preparing dinner and keeping watch for any possible trouble, entered at this point to give her opinion. "Jim, I don't think there's a right or a wrong answer to your question. Doesn't it indicate in the gospels that when the abomination of desolation occurs that the believers ought to flee for the mountains? At the same time, which one of us would fault the brother who risks his freedom and life to proclaim the Gospel to one who is dying in sin, and who has so little time now to repent? On a personal level, Jim, I think you are more important right now outside of jail rather than inside of it. This paper that you are going to prepare, with discretion, needs to go much farther than the hands of Rev. Irving. It should reach the hands of as many believers as possible."

"As should the letter of Pastor Samuels," added Sandy.

Jim read Pastor Samuel's letter again for the sake of John Dunn and Malcolm Ivy.

"Yes, there does seem to be a place for both of you," said Malcolm. "The prisoner pastor and the fugitive pastor."

"But what about us?" questioned Steve Brown, almost as much in the form of a comment as a question. "For now we are free. Why should we keep trying to accumulate riches? Any money or properties we gain now will be useless when the antichrist establishes his cashless society. I have no doubt that by that time the United States will be part of the Global Union. This is our last window of opportunity to be a testimony to those around us. We must seize the moment, while it is still here."

"And what about preparing for when the antichrist declares himself to be God?" asked John Dunn. "We must have a safe place to go and food to eat."

"Any attempts to make such plans as a group runs the risk of discovery," Sven replied. "When the Global Union puts on the pressure, many of those whom we thought were brothers will turn into betrayers. I suspect that inside our small group of believers in Green Bluff there is at least one traitor. Somehow information leaks out to those who are against the cause of Christ. This letter that you have from Pastor Samuels is the last that he was able to send out of the jail. It somehow got into the hands of Sam Johansen, who by protesting to the town council, succeeded in having any future letters stopped. I think someone in our congregation, with malicious intent, gave it to him."

"So we can make plans, but we shouldn't do it as a church or tell others what those plans are," John persisted.

"Well, we need to help one another, but, yes, I think that would be the wisest plan of action," counseled Sven.

"I think you're right," John agreed, already making plans inside his head.

They talked on for another 20 minutes or so, making concrete plans of how to proceed from there. They finished with a time of fervent prayer. They prayed for strength and faithfulness. They prayed for the lost. They prayed that the Lord would help them in their plans to strengthen and encourage other believers, and that He would give them boldness in their witness for Jesus.

Following prayer, John and Malcolm said their good-byes, while the Browns and the Svensens stayed on for dinner and a time of lighter fellowship after the meal.

"Do you think John can be trusted?" Sven asked Jim privately, as they watched John and Malcolm drive away. "He seemed most interested in his own personal survival."

"Time will tell," replied Jim.

Chapter 14

Sam Johansen was furious when he looked at the anonymous pamphlet. The explosive nature of his anger frightened his son, Lance.

"Where is he?" Sam demanded.

"I don't know, Dad. Honest I don't. Elder Svensen brought these to the meeting on Friday night, saying that Pastor had written them. He said that he and Elder Brown have met several times with Pastor Jim, and that he and his family are well. When asked where they were living, they said that they thought it was best not to say, as they suspected that there might be one or more traitors in the group."

"I won't have you calling that man 'Pastor' in my presence. He is a deceiver. Call him Deceiver."

"Do you think he was referring to me, Dad, when he talked of traitors?"

"You're not a traitor, Son," answered his dad, gaining control over his anger. Putting his arm around his son, he continued, "You're doing what I ask you to do and you're doing what is right. Deceiver has the rest of them brainwashed or they would have turned him in already. Isn't it true that the law is after him? You haven't told anybody about meeting with me?"

"They know that we see one another from time to time, but no one knows that I've been telling you about the church meetings. They're supposed to be secret."

"Good. Make sure nobody finds out what you are telling me, especially your mom."

"Why don't you let us come back home, Dad," urged Lance, "and you start going back to the church. I want to be a family again."

"It's too late for that son. Until Deceiver is caught and jailed, your mom and the church will never be right. After that, you can come and live with me if you want. Until that time, I need you to stay where you are and to give me all the information you can find out.

Okay, son? I'm counting on you. Don't lie or hold out on me. You're pretty good friends with the Brown girl, aren't you? See if you can get her to tell you anything about where Deceiver might be, but don't let her know why you want to know. Times are confusing, son. You have to trust me that what you are doing is right. We are in this together for the good of our family and the church. Don't let me down."

"Dad, could you give us some money?" asked Lance. "The church people have been helping some, but things are pretty tight right now."

Thinking about it for a minute, Sam looked directly into his son's eyes, and replied: "Lance, you can do with this money what you wish, but I want you to know that I'm giving it to you, not to your mother, and I'm giving it to you because we are working together. She'll ask questions, so be careful how you spend it." Sam went into a back room of the house and returned with an envelope which he gave to Lance. "There will more where this came from if you can help me find the Deceiver. Let's see one another again soon," said Sam, giving his son a hug.

Outside, Lance was amazed to find $1,000.00 in the envelope which his dad had given him.

After his son left, Sam's effort at a pleasant demeanor disappeared completely. The nearest lamp went flying and crashed against the opposite wall as a stream of expletives erupted from his mouth.

It was not really necessary that Lance surrender a copy of the pamphlet into the hands of his dad. Within a week, the pamphlet was widely distributed throughout the town, as well as the information about its authorship. It was the talk of the town for many a day. In the two weeks that it had taken him to write it, Jim had done an excellent job of presenting biblical facts, current events, and practical applications for both the believer and for the unbeliever. He did not mince his words. To the unbeliever, he stated clearly that to turn to Christ now would mean imprisonment and death within a matter of months. To refuse to do so would result no less in suffering, and would mean, as well, eternal peril for the soul. Jim detailed the events which would soon take place, and encouraged all to acknowledge the truth of God's Word when they did. "Whatever you do, do not bow down before and worship the Supreme Leader as God. It is better to starve than to receive his mark," he warned. Although the Global Union's moving to a cashless economy had been announced, nothing about the plans to declare the Supreme Leader to be the Most High God, much less the specifics about doing it in the Temple of Jerusalem, had been mentioned. The Bible and Jim's pamphlet had the global scoop on the story.

The believers were encouraged to stand strong under persecution and to realize that members of their own church bodies and families would turn against them in the last days. Without using Sam's name, Jim recounted his own story of Sam's betrayal and Sam's wrath against him and the whole church. If believers felt led by God to prepare hideaways and stock them with food for when the abomination of desolation occurred, they were encouraged to do so, but secretly and in small groups. As far as Jim could figure it, the church had a matter of a few months, maximum, to be able to win the lost for Jesus. More than ever before, this needed to become the focus of every believer. Pastor Samuel's final letter from his jail cell was included in the pamphlet.

The believers in Green Bluff were indeed strengthened in the faith and emboldened in their witness by what Jim and Peter had written. The promise of Jesus in Revelation 2:10 became their rallying cry: "Fear none of those things which you will suffer... be faithful unto death, and I will give you a crown of life."

Tom Watson smiled at receiving a copy in a town hall meeting. He rejoiced that his friend had not been silenced, and that he was apparently alive and well.

Peter Samuels read his own words with tears of joy. How great God was to be able to reach down into the jail of Green Bluff and to use him in such a mighty way.

Sam Johansen became the despised man of the town. Though not named, everyone soon knew who he was. Though there were many who were not sympathetic to the Christian message, few respected a traitor. Sam was mocked almost everywhere he went. "Hey, Sam, you betray a friend today?" "Jesus is fine in the good times, but not so great in the bad. Maybe secretly you're still one of his followers." People seemed to forget his real name, and began referring to him as

Judas. It didn't help that during his many years as a "Christian" Sam had acted self-righteous in his contact with "sinners." It was pitiable. Ronald Smith tried to reach out to him, saying that Jesus and the church were ready to forgive and receive him back, but Sam would have none of it. Sam withdrew into himself, avoiding contact with others as much as he was able. His story ended tragically. On December 25, his wife, son, and daughter went to see him at the house. The doors were locked and the curtains drawn. Using her key, Ellen opened the door and called out to Sam. There was no answer. Searching the house, Lance found his dad in the bathroom. An open bottle of whiskey lay tipped on its side on the sink counter. Jim's pamphlet lay torn and strewn about the room. Sam lay in a pool of his own blood with a pistol in his hand.

What took place with the pamphlets outside of Green Bluff was one of those unforeseen and unexpected events of history. When Jim met with the others on November 9th at the Peterson farm, the idea was that he would write up his scriptural conclusions for the benefit and use of the two churches represented there in the dining room. Divine destiny had other plans. Nobody was sure how it happened, but Jim's writings began to be reproduced and distributed by the hundreds of thousands. It was not anything even remotely foreseen, and it was impossible that it could have been planned. It just happened. Copies fell into the hands of Christian printers who dedicated their time and resources to its reproduction. Nobody worried about copyrights. The writing was anonymous, and besides, there was no time to think about such petty concerns. Informal underground distribution methods sprang up almost overnight. In the states where the believers still had freedom of movement, copies were being handed out to passersby on the street corners. Other brothers dedicated themselves to its translation into other languages. Believers, at the risk of their lives, traveled abroad and left packages of the pamphlets where they would be found and read. By the end of January 2020, what had been hundreds of thousands of copies reached into the millions, and a pamphlet originally written in a small farm house in Wisconsin by an unknown fugitive pastor, reached the hands and the attention of the Supreme Leader of the Global Community.

The Supreme Leader was a cool character. He made decisions with ease and very few occurrences seemed to take him by surprise. Jim's pamphlet, "A Christian View on Current Times and Events," was an unexpected problem, and he didn't like unexpected problems. The Supreme Leader began to lose his composure as he read Jim's writing. He hated Christians. He couldn't control them. For that reason, he had spent so much effort trying to eliminate them. He asked his aides to leave the room. He paced as he read, pounding his desk from time to time in anger. How could this have happened? How had his plans about Jerusalem leaked out? The author detailed everything about the plans that they had made except to mention the day and the hour. "Damn," he yelled, throwing the pamphlet against a chair. He would find out how it happened and who was behind it. He would find out who the author was and why he had so far escaped from jail and death. As soon as he did, he would remedy the situation.

What kind of effect would this book have? He hated the idea that many might refuse to bow and worship him because of what this writer had revealed. How had so many copies been printed and distributed when such literature had been strictly banned? Would he have to change his plans now so as not to appear a fool?

He grabbed his phone and dialed Pope Adrian's number. The Supreme Leader avoided the pleasantries. "Get me Pope Adrian. This is the Supreme Leader. It's an emergency.

Hello, Adrian. Are you aware of a little booklet entitled, "A Christian View of Current Times and Events?"

"I am, my Lord."

"You are, my Lord! Well, where does it come from? Who leaked out our plans?"

"My Lord," replied Adrian, in a difficult spot, "I am aware of no leaks as to our plans to declare you "God, the Most High." You will be aware, however, that the Christian Scriptures seem to prophesy, with remarkable clarity, the great event to which we are looking forward. But be assured, most people have long ago given up believing in any literal fulfillment of those words which were written so long ago."

"Be assured? You want me to be assured? Somebody believes those words and now a lot of people believe in them. Let me get this

107

right," the Supreme Leader calculated through his clenched teeth, venom dripping from every word, "you suggested to me a plan that fulfills the prophesies of your precious book? Do you take me for a fool? Am I now your puppet? You will find very soon that your puppet will not be very manageable in your hands."

"Do I need to affirm again to you my loyalty? I have no other god except you. What you call my precious book, has not been so precious to me. It was for my neglect of it that I failed to foresee this problem. We suggested the plan of declaring you to be God at your orders. You wanted a religion that would unite the world's peoples instead of dividing them. This was the best plan we could think of, not to mention the only feasible one available. Why does one foolish little book concern you so?"

"This foolish little book, from what I understand, would be a worldwide best seller, if it were permitted to be published and sold legally. We cannot afford to have our plans openly declared and opposed before we have the chance to even announce them!"

"I will look, my Lord, for any leaks among the committee members, but I assure you, these men and women, be it out of devotion or fear, are loyal to you. What we could do, however, is declare a leak. This book is so famous and widely received because its author claims that it is based on divine revelation. If the events occur, as he says the Bible has foretold, then it is possible that many will rebel against us. If, however, we can convince people that his information did not come from God but from a leak from within the ecumenical committee, than he will be discredited, and we can turn this situation to our own advantage. Send your media people down here to get quotes from those of us who serve on the committee. We will be able to phrase things in such a way that the world will know that what is planned for Easter Day was not revealed by God, but by a loose-lipped human. If we are careful to do it right, we may be successful in stirring up a renewed vigor to wipe out these troublesome fanatics."

There was silence, as the Supreme leader considered what Pope Adrian proposed. He broke the silence with a laugh. "I like talking to you Adrian. You're devious. If you hadn't gone the route of religion you would have made an excellent politician. Are we ready to openly reveal our plans concerning the world religion of which I

"Another couple of weeks preparation would have been preferable," answered Pope Adrian, "but circumstances dictate that we should move now."

"I don't like circumstances dictating what I do, Adrian. I like dictating the circumstances. But you are right. Prepare your people. The reporters will arrive in a matter of hours. In the meantime, I will find out who our anonymous author is and put an end to the growing distribution of his writings. Keep me informed, and, Adrian, don't double-cross me. I don't need to tell you what will happen to you, if I find out that you are working against me instead of for me."

When he hung up the phone, the Supreme Leader was visibly more relaxed. He called for his aides to return to the room and asked for his security counsel to be called together for an emergency meeting.

109

Chapter 15

Following the release of Jim's pamphlets, the police made several visits to the Peterson home. Each time, the Allens were successfully whisked out of sight before the officers were able to see them. The Petersons did not lie about where their daughter and son-in-law were; they simply refused to answer any questions regarding them. As the police did not come with search warrants, they were not allowed beyond the back porch. It was clear, however, that the authorship of the pamphlets had not remained totally anonymous, and that a different plan would have to be devised for their safety. Camping was out of the question, as winter had settled in to stay for awhile. In addition to the cold, all of the foliage had fallen and the campsite was too visible from the field. Mr. Peterson had taken down the tent some weeks earlier.

For the time being they decided to build a false wall in one of the bedrooms. Mr. Peterson bought the building materials from a supply house some 40 minutes from his farm, so as not to arouse local suspicion. The room was small, 2½ feet by 8 feet. Two old mattresses were put in, in case it was necessary to sleep there; a portable toilet; some reading materials; some cold food stocks; and a couple of games. Its entrance was a small crawl hole under a bed. The bedroom, with its new wall, was papered in a pattern similar to what had previously been on the walls and the kids had fun helping their parents and grandparents make it look old. Carol couldn't believe that her grandmother really wanted her to write on the wall with crayon. Caleb had the privilege of purposefully spilling a glass of grape juice on it. When they were done, it looked as if the wall paper had been up for several years. Careful inspection of the wall behind the bed revealed the entrance to the hideaway, but the Petersons and the Allens hoped that no one would be so thorough. An electric line was strung through from the neighboring room for light.

After the hideaway was completed, the Petersons ran the Allens through many a police drill. They were ruthless, sometimes even waking the Allens up in the middle of the night. Mr. Peterson played the role of the observant policeman, finding the clues left behind by the family that made him suspicious of the Allen's presence. It became a game to see how fast they could escape into their hideaway without leaving a trace that they had been living in the house. New habits were learned, such as eating meals without plates, silverware, or glasses. Soon everyone in the family knew what his or her responsibility was in the case of a police raid.

Their caution was not without reason. The news headlines for January 28th read, "The Global Union Seeks Knowledge Concerning the Identity and Whereabouts of the Anonymous Author of 'A Christian View of Current Times and Events.'" At 3:45 p.m. that day, Officer Grady arrived with three other policemen and four FBI agents.

Duke announced their arrival.

Mrs. Peterson was quick to lock the back door.

Mr. Peterson came out from the barn, calling off Duke and putting on a hard of hearing act, which was not hard to do as he had placed plugs in his ears.

The officers fanned out, as Officer Grady approached Mr. Peterson. "Mr. Peterson... Mr. Peterson."

"I'm sorry, I can't hear you son."

"Mr. Peterson, we're here with a search warrant," Officer Grady said raising his voice.

"Just a minute, Officer, I'll tie up old Duke here, and then maybe I can hear what you have to say."

Mr. Peterson led Duke to his run with Officer Grady following.

"Mr. Peterson, we're here with a search warrant," repeated Officer Grady, practically yelling.

"These blasted things," said Mr. Peterson, pulling out the plugs. "You can't be too careful with your hearing. Now what is it that you wanted to say?"

"We're here with a search warrant!"

"Okay, okay. You don't have to yell. Is there some escaped convict around the area?"

"You know very well who we're looking for Mr. Peterson. We've come to search your house and property, and we expect your full cooperation."

"Where's the search warrant?" Mr. Peterson asked.

"Here it is," replied Officer Grady.

"Yes, indeed, it is a search warrant. You've come better prepared this time, Mr. Grady. Have a look around if you like. I'll let Mrs. Peterson know that you're here.

One minute and fourteen seconds. It was four seconds off their record time, but they made it into their hideaway with about a minute and a half to spare.

An hour and a half later the agents left the farm, not quite empty handed. They had found Jim's car back in the old garbage dump. It was obvious that it had been there for some time. The snow on the ground impeded them from impounding the car, so they simply removed some of its parts to make it difficult for it to be used again.

"You told us," Officer Grady said angrily to Mrs. Peterson, "that your son-in-law picked up his family and drove away."

"So I did," replied Mrs. Peterson, "but I did not tell you where they drove to, did I? If you are looking for me to give you information of any kind, you are going to be sadly frustrated."

"You're playing a very dangerous game, Mrs. Peterson. If you are found to be harboring a fugitive, you, too, will be arrested."

"Officer Grady, you do know how to sweet talk a woman. Have you given any more thought of your need to accept Jesus as your Savior and Lord?"

"We will see each other again, Mrs. Peterson." With that the officers left.

Mr. Peterson took a ride that night in his car. He stopped to greet one of the FBI officers who was parked on the hill overlooking the farm. "It's a lovely, clear night tonight. I see you like to look at the stars with your binoculars. Have a good evening, Officer."

The next raid came at 3:00 am the following morning. The Petersons and the Allens were ready. Duke announced the arrival of their visitors. Mr. Peterson, who had been watching a late night movie on television in the kitchen, saw their arrival before he heard

Duke's barking. The children were already comfortably asleep in the secret room. Jim and Sandy, awakened by Mr. Peterson, quickly made their bed and made their way into the hideaway. Mrs. Peterson did a survey of the room and picked up anything that might be out of place. Meanwhile, Mr. Peterson fumbled with the door lock downstairs to let in Officer Grady and three others.

"My, Officer Grady, you're working late tonight," quipped Mr. Peterson.

Handing him a paper, the law enforcement officers pushed their way past Mr. Peterson without a word. Mr. Peterson didn't bother to look at it. He knew it was another search warrant. An hour and fifteen minutes later, they left, this time with some new information which they would find to be very interesting. Two of the officers on the early morning visit were finger print experts. They carefully dusted for prints in many of the rooms of the house. Of course, many of the prints were found later that day to match with the prints of Jim and Sandy and their children.

Surely they had been found out. Why hadn't they thought about finger prints? When the police and FBI left, Jim, Sandy, and the Petersons held a counsel of war in the bedroom by the hiding place. Time was short. The officers, no doubt, would return as soon as they had opportunity to compare the fingerprints. This time they would not leave until they led Jim, and likely the Petersons, away with them, in handcuffs.

"Well, we'll have to leave as quick as we can, while it's still dark," said Jim.

"We can't," replied Mr. Peterson. "They're watching the house. They'll stop any vehicle leaving the property."

"I'll have to take off on foot alone, then," said Jim. "After all, it's me that they're after."

"I'm afraid it's not that simple anymore," said Mrs. Peterson. "When they find that the prints they dusted for are yours, they will arrest Dad and me for aiding and abetting a fugitive. Officer Grady has been looking for an excuse to arrest us for some time now. This will be more than sufficient motive."

"Well, what do we do?" asked Sandy.

All were silent for several minutes.

"It's not a good idea, but it's the only one I can think of," said

Mr. Peterson, breaking the silence.

"Well what is it?" encouraged his wife. "Any idea is better than none."

"I hope so," said Mr. Peterson, still doubtful. "The idea is this. You all leave on foot in about half-an-hour, the sooner the better, heading up through the fields to Durmont Road. That includes you, Helen. It will still be dark, and they might not see you. At about 7:30, I'll load up the horse trailer with a couple of cows and pull it with the pick up. When they stop me, I'll be alone which hopefully will arouse less suspicion. I will tell them that I am taking the cows over to the Harvester farm. You know how they lost a lot of their cows in a fire recently. If, and it's a big if, if they don't follow me, I will swing around to Durmont Road, we'll let the cows loose and load everybody up. What I don't know, is where we should go from there."

"We'll have the ask the Lord's help, so that they don't follow you," Jim observed. "It's our only chance. If they don't follow you, how much time do you think we would have before they start looking for the truck and the trailer? It seems now that the Supreme Leader is in on the chase. I feel like his number one priority."

"It all depends on when they can get solid confirmation about the finger prints and another search warrant issued by a judge. I'd say we would probably have about three hours, at least," guessed Mr. Peterson. "They shouldn't be in any rush, as they are watching the farm."

"I don't think we should take anything for granted," added Mrs. Peterson.

"This may sound insane," said Sandy, "but didn't Sven tell you, Dad, that Sam Johansen committed suicide on Christmas day. The Johansen house is a large one, and as far as we know, nobody is staying there. Ellen would certainly consent to let us use it."

"That would be the perfect place," agreed Jim. "Who would think of looking for us there? Sam was my greatest enemy. Ellen could make trips to the house with things that we would need, and nobody would think anything of it."

"Well, that settles it," concluded Mr. Peterson. "The clock is running. We should wake up the kids and get everybody started with a good breakfast. Only bring the bare essentials, as you will have to carry them. Remember lots of warm blankets, as it will be cold for those driving back in the horse trailer. We'll call up the parsonage and the Svensen's house at a pay phone along the way. Let's hope they're there. I think that we shouldn't bring the truck and trailer into Green Bluff. Maybe we could ditch it along the way and have Sven pick us up in his cargo van."

"That's a good idea, Dad," said Jim. "I know just the place to meet him."

"What about the animals?" asked Mrs. Peterson.

"I'll have to call somebody to watch them. Watch them, no. We'll never be farming again. Maybe the Harvesters will get some cows out of this after all."

After several minutes of joint prayer, they swung into action.

The escape plan worked to perfection. Truth be told, the policeman doing surveillance had given up interest in watching the dark farmhouse that didn't seem to be going anywhere, and began to pay more attention to a magazine he had brought along. In any case, it would have been difficult to see the small group of three adults and three children slipping away in the darkness of the pre-dawn hour.

He did notice Mr. Peterson heading out to the barn at about 7:00 am, but this was not unusual for a farmer. At 7:30, however, his full attention was aroused at seeing a truck pulling a horse trailer leave the Peterson driveway. Radioing headquarters of what was taking place, the officer was instructed to stop the vehicles and inspect them, calling headquarters again before letting the vehicles proceed.

Mr. Peterson was convincing, particularly as the officer on duty happened to be a cousin of the Harvester family. After a thorough check of the vehicles, the officer radioed the station: "It's only Mr. Peterson taking two cows as a gift to help replenish the Harvester herd. Several of the farmers in the area are helping in this way."

"Are you sure there is no one else in the truck nor the trailer?" quizzed the dispatcher.

"Positive. Do you want me to detain him?"

"On what grounds? On the grounds of being a good neighbor? No, let him go, and keep watch on the house."

"Yes, sir, Sergeant." With that, the officer apologized to Mr. Peterson and said he was free to go. He ended with, "Have a good day!"

"Thank you," Mr. Peterson replied sincerely, directing his words as much to God as to the officer. "I think it will be a good one."

Four hours later, it was an angry group of policemen and federal officials who found an unoccupied farm house, six sets of tracks leading out into the snow covered fields, and a secret room which the Petersons and the Allens had not bothered any longer to hide. The local officers and agents did not know who was putting on the pressure for Jim Allen's arrest. They knew it was somebody big, and they knew that he or she would not be very happy. Police throughout the state were notified to be on the alert for the pickup truck and trailer, but it was too late. The Petersons and Allens were already safely enjoying the hospitality of Ellen Johansen.

Chapter 16

In other parts of the country, the question as to what to do with religious intolerance was far from resolved. Under pressure from the Global Union, and with the enthusiastic support of many anti-God lawmakers, the United States had passed and begun to implement the "Unity and Acceptance of Faith Act." From the start, it was controversial and was applied unevenly throughout the country. If the early days of the law were confusing, it was even more so in January of 2020.

South Carolina had become an armed camp. Christians from throughout the country had indeed fled there. The governor of the state, without formally declaring independence, saw the future and began to prepare for it. If the federal government was going to deny the principles upon which the United States was founded, his state would be one in which they would continued to be upheld. Since June, he had the citizens of South Carolina preparing for the war which was to come, including arms production, military training, defense works along the borders, and the stockpiling of needed provisions. Border crossings had been established at every entrance into the state. Matters came to a head in the early part of January, when National Guard forces took charge of the military bases located on South Carolina soil. It was a nearly bloodless take over. Military forces not in agreement with the South Carolina government were escorted to the border. All military equipment was confiscated for use by what was now being called the State Militia. The Federal Government, undecided up to that point as to how to react to the South Carolina situation, responded swiftly by sealing off the borders. Seeing the failure of their efforts to try and topple the state's government from within, all citizens who opposed South Carolina's rebellion against the Federal Government were encouraged to leave the state by February 8th. It was a prelude to war. South Carolina's Governor Early was all too happy to let the traitors go, providing public transportation for them to the border.

The situation in Alabama was similar to that of South Carolina but had not yet reached the explosive proportions of the conflict there.

Other states, overburdened with the costs of housing the hundreds of thousands of new prisoners who refused to deny their religious faith, saw themselves obligated to set the majority of them at liberty again.

California, using a creative interpretation of racketeering laws, seized the assets of jailed Christians, Jews, and Muslims to compensate the state for the costs of their imprisonment. Other states seemed poised to adopt this same measure.

What had not been accepted, though fought for by many, was the Global Union's solution of murdering the unrepentant.

It was clear that the federal government was going to need to do more than simply make a law and expect that the states would implement it. What was needed was a concrete plan on the federal level, along with the political will to implement it in a nationally uniform way.

The federal government, however, was working on a much bigger issue than this, and one which had the immediate potential of solving the religious problem. An agreement was close at hand, whereby the United States Government would yield its authority and sovereignty over to the Global Union. Most of the younger generations of Americans had grown up being bottle fed the advantages of globalization and the need for a new world order. What had made America so slow in integrating itself into the Global Union had been the ever present American pride that it would be America who would lead the way and hold the reins. It was obvious now to all, that was not going to be the case, and that if America did not jump on board now, it would become isolated from the rest of the world. What the politicians had been striving for was the best deal that they could get from the Union. They wanted to be a part of the Union while maintaining a political and national autonomy. On this point, there was no negotiation. To enter the Global Union was to lose your identity as a nation. The Union's laws became your laws. National resources became property of the Global Union for the good of all. When the Union refused to budge on the issue of autonomy, the

United States' politicians argued for a continued role in administration and policy making. At this point, their efforts were purely selfish. They were not looking out for the good of the nation, but trying to assure themselves of ongoing employment. In this, the Union was more than ready to negotiate. If the United States' leaders were willing to accept the Union's conditions, swear loyalty to the Supreme Leader, and agree to implement all of its edicts, then there would certainly be a job for them under the Global Union's administration of the nation.

What was problematic was how to bring about this transfer of government to a foreign power. The United States Constitution addressed how the nation was to go to war, but it did not address how it might surrender without a fight. Such a matter had been inconceivable to the founders of the nation. There was no legal ground to stand on. There was no procedure to follow. There was no national precedent to use as a model. And what was more, the governmental leaders were not sure that they could even count on a majority vote of the citizens to support such a matter. The fact that the Supreme Leader had decided that he would set himself up as "God Most High" did not help. The Americans laughed that he had been scooped on the story by some unknown author. Most Americans were not ready to bow down and worship anyone, much less another human being. America at its birth had fought to rid itself from a "Supreme Leader" and that spirit of independence was still strong. "To hell with the Global Union and the Supreme Leader," was the attitude of many. If the conspirators did not yield authority to the Global Union in the right way, they could find their plans frustrated and themselves out of a job, if not lynched as traitors.

After much talk and too many leaks to the press, the president and his advisors made the decision that it was time to act and to act boldly. He would not count on the opinion or approval of the American people. He felt sure that he had the votes in Congress to pass a measure yielding the Sovereignty of the United States over to Global Union. The military was divided, but he knew who he could count on for support and who he could not. Most in high command had been schooled in globalism and had been appreciative of the relative peace which the world was enjoying through the military intervention of the Global Union. For many years, American soldiers had worn the colors of a foreign commanded global force, in fighting as part of the United Nations Peace Keeping Force. Many would not find it difficult to change uniforms to fight as part of the Global Force for Unity and Peace. If there was any trouble, Global Union forces would be on hand to deal with it.

Within a matter of six days everything was prepared. The United States Government would stage a "legal" anti-coup. Instead of seizing power unconstitutionally through military force, they would be yielding up authority by the very same means. February 14th was the date set. Though some rumors had spread regarding what might take place, few who opposed the idea took them with seriousness or urgency. Those who did found themselves being laughed at as alarmists, and shut out by most of the major news organizations.

On the night of February 13th, leading members of the House and Senate, the Chiefs of Staff, representatives of the Global Union, select member of the press, and the Presidential Cabinet, met with the President in the White House. There were some who were not there. For example, the highest ranking general in the Air Force and the Senate opposition leader had not received invitations. The meeting lasted two hours. At the end of the meeting, the President offered a toast in honor of an expanded Global Union and to the health of the Supreme Leader. This was followed by a warning to all those present, that the Supreme Leader himself would deal as he saw fit, with anyone who might be so foolish as to betray the plans that had been laid that night. "Gentlemen, as of tomorrow night, the United States will no longer exist as a political entity, and I will no longer be your President."

The following morning after the House roll call, Speaker Thomas announced, "The House agenda for today is being suspended due to a matter of supreme national interest and by the request of the President. Today, I place before you a bill that has been seconded by the minority whip. Special rules of order will be applied to it. Fifteen minutes will be allowed for questions to clarify the nature of the bill. This will be followed by a period of debate lasting no longer than an hour, with interventions not to exceed three minutes each. Following this period of debate, we will immediately vote on the matter. Due to the importance and urgency of the bill, any member who is seen to be out of order, will be asked to leave the hall. Copies of the bill are now being distributed to you."

The minority leader flashed a questioning look to his whip, who avoided eye contact with him.

When all the copies were distributed, Speaker Thomas began again, "I will now read the bill."

"Treason," yelled Representative Fisher, from Alabama, standing to his feet. "This is treason."

"Will the representative from Alabama please take his seat and allow the bill to be read," requested Speaker Thomas.

Murmurs began to sweep the hall as other members read the bill before them.

"I will not sit down. This bill is treason, and I will not sit down while the Constitution of the United States is being violated and our nation's sovereignty is threatened."

"Nor I," replied a second representative from Alabama. Several others in the hall rose to their feet and added their voices in protest.

"Gentlemen, there will be a time for questions and debate on this issue. If you will sit down, we can proceed with this matter in an orderly manner," reasoned the speaker.

"There is nothing to debate, Mr. Speaker," continued Representative Fisher. "The words are plain, as has been your disregard for House rules this morning. Mr. Speaker, that you would present before us such a bill is evidence of your part in plotting against the government of our great nation. It is I, Mr. Speaker, who demand that you stand down."

Speaker Thomas banged his hammer on the podium, trying to get the attention of the members who were quickly turning the hall into a mob scene. "I will ask you again, Mr. Fisher, and those who are standing with you, to sit down and hold your peace. If you will not I have no other alternative than to hold you in contempt of the House and ask the officers to take you out of the hall. In this case you will lose both voice and vote in the matter at hand."

Representative Fisher looked around the hall and noticed the vastly increased police presence there on that day. He normally knew most of the officers but today very few faces were familiar. He glanced towards the press core. The opposite was true there. Only a handful of reporters were present. Where were the rest? Suddenly it became very clear to him. "I beg the pardon of the Speaker and my fellow members. I had a bit of an argument with my wife this morning, and came here ready for the same." His attempt at humor had its desired effect, as many responded with nervous laughter. "I ask my colleagues to sit as the Speaker has requested. If you would pardon me, I will go to the bathroom and splash a bit of water on my face and attempt to return for the debate in a more reasonable mood."

"Certainly," responded the Speaker, expecting nothing out of the ordinary.

The members who had stood with Fisher were struck dumb by his reversal of attitude, and sat down sheepishly. They would speak, they reasoned, but during the time allotted for debate. Certainly this measure could not pass.

Representative Fisher knew it would pass. His hope was to head it off before it reached the Senate. He did go to the bathroom and then headed for the exit to the street instead of for the House floor. He was stopped at the door on his way out by a police officer he did not know, asking for his identification. "I'm sorry, Mr. Fisher, House members are being asked to stay today until some very important bills are dealt with."

"I see," Fisher responded, "but I'm out of cigarettes and I always buy them at the corner news stand. I'll be right back."

"I'm sorry, Mr. Fisher, I have my orders."

"You have misunderstood your orders. House members have never been forced to be present, even in the most important of votes. If my constituents don't like it that I stepped out, they can vote for somebody else next time."

"I am not permitted to let you leave the building, Mr. Fisher," replied the officer resolutely.

"And I am not about to tolerate such foolishness. May I see you badge officer? I would like to record its number and your name."

The officer showed him his badge. Representative Fisher purposefully bumped it out of his hand. As the officer bent to pick it up, Fisher gave him a shove that sent him sprawling, and ran out of the building. Running down the Capitol steps and through a crowd of highschoolers who had come to tour the Capitol building. Fisher kept ahead of the pursuing police officers. Crossing First Street, he outdistanced his would be captures, and lost them as he passed

124

through a large crowd of protesters in front of the Supreme Court building. The police were quickly at his heels, but he lost them, running through the traffic, and disappearing into the crowd on the busy streets.

Fisher was frantic. He had so little time. The phone, he would use his phone. He called everybody he could think of calling, beginning with his friend, Governor Applebee of Alabama. Governor Applebee had hoped that the United States wouldn't unite with the Global Union, but had rightly expected that it would probably be just a matter of time. He had asked Fisher to alert him as soon as events headed in that direction. Alerted by Fisher, Governor Applebee, who had been reluctant to break away from the United States as South Carolina had done, had no such qualms about pulling out of the Global Union, to which he had never agreed to be a part. He would contact who he could to try to prevent what was happening in Washington, but communicated to Fisher that most of his efforts would be directed towards defending the people of Alabama.

Fisher was beginning his second term in the House. As he flipped through his electronic directory calling anyone and everyone who might be able to help, he wished that he had spent more energy during his first term forming a network of friends and establishing influence in Washington. His hope was to raise up in one hour an army of protesters that would storm the Senate chambers and forbid any consideration whatsoever that day of the bill which he was sure would pass in the House. If the people of America could know, and have time to respond, the events, which the Speaker and whoever else had planned, might be stopped. The rumors that had been floating about were true, but how could he convince a sufficient number of protesters in such a short time? In the end, he couldn't. News organizations would not go on air with his revelations, as they were unconfirmed and uncorroborated. The homeless and leftist groups, the ones most likely to turn out on short notice, were largely in favor of joining with the Global Union. Fisher's was a voice crying in the wilderness, and there were few who cared to listen or pay attention to what he had to say. In the end, some 130 protesters showed up outside of the Capitol building to protest, far fewer than what were necessary to do any good.

The House bill read, "In favor of union with the Global Union, with all the benefits that such a union would bring about for the American people, on this day, February 14th, 2020, with the passage of this bill into law, we, the Congress and President of the United States, in representation of the citizenry who elected us, declare an end, effective immediately, to the United States of America, yielding our national sovereignty, together with our personal and natural resources, over to the governing power of the Global Union."

The measure passed in the House and Senate by comfortable margins, and was signed into law by the President at 1:45 pm that same day.

The announcement of the federal government's dissolution in favor of union with the Global Union was met by many and varied responses. A significant part of the population responded to the news with great jubilation. Spontaneous street parties sprang up throughout the nation, celebrating the good news of a greater involvement with the world community. Others rose up in protest. These protests were quickly controlled or suppressed in the major cities by a strong police and military presence. Others, concerned neither with the United States nor the Global Union, but seeing their opportunity, rioted, smashing store windows and carrying away what they could. The most significant response to the announcement came from large segments of the Air Force. In response to what they saw as a clear and illegal takeover of the country on the part of the politicians of the nation, they bombed the White House, the Capitol Building, and the Pentagon. Were it not for the strong support of the generals of the other branches of the military, such a response might have resulted in a reversal of the decisions of the day. As it was, it turned out to be a last angry defiance of what was to be. The President had not expected such a quick and decisive response from General Brady, though he knew the Air Force commander to be firmly against the loss of national sovereignty. Responding quickly, however, he gained ground control of the air bases, and prevented any further sorties by the airborne branch of the military. He did not do it, however, before some 250 military aircraft, much of which was the most sophisticated and advanced that the military had to offer, found their way to the southern states of South Carolina and Alabama.

Be that as it may, the clock could not be turned back now. Global Union military forces had already crossed the border from Canada and Mexico and were taking up strategic positions. The political and military anti-coup had been effective. The United States was no more.

Chapter 17

News of the Global Union's takeover of the United States, greeted with enthusiasm by many, was not good news for Christians. What had been a confused and uneven persecution of believers up to that point, would now be very specific, defined, and universal.

It took nearly two weeks for the Global Union to establish order and rule over most of its new territory and population. During this time they were too busy to be much concerned as to what to do with religious extremists. By February 27th, however, the Global Union made clear what their course of action would be. Those who were currently imprisoned for reasons of religious bigotry would be given two weeks time in which they might repent, the same time granted at that moment to all citizens throughout the Global Union. At the end of those two weeks, those who would stubbornly refuse to repent of their religious extremism and acknowledge the validity of all faiths and lifestyles would be beheaded. That two week period was also meant as a period of clemency for those who had not yet been imprisoned for their faith. In that time, they, too, were seriously encouraged to acknowledge the errors of their beliefs and ways. At the end of the two week period, new arrests would be made.

Tom Watson arrived at the Green Bluff jail on March 1st for his weekly visit with Pastor Samuels. Many visits back, Tom had dropped the formalities and begun to refer to his friend and brother as Peter. Yes, a conversion had taken place, but it was not the one that the town councilmen had imagined.

Tom was long faced as he entered the interrogation room, where he and Peter had met since their first jail visit together. There, already seated, was Pastor Samuels, who rose to greet his guest.

When the door had been shut, Peter asked, "Why so solemn?"

"Haven't you heard the news?" replied Tom.

"You mean that the Packers star running back will miss all of next season because of a knee injury?" quipped Peter dryly.

"How is it that you can still joke at a time like as this?" asked Tom, more in exasperation than truly wanting to know.

"The joy of the Lord is my strength and my sure hope is that I shall soon be seeing Him face to face. I believe the fifteenth or the sixteenth to be the day. Don't grieve for me or yourself Tom. Grieve for those who because of their hatred and unbelief will put us to death. Grieve for those who will not lose their heads because they have never surrendered their hearts to Christ. He is the only one who can save them from an eternity of separation from God and from all that is good. Grieve and pray for them, Tom. Ours is a glorious fate. I've been wondering about you, though, Tom. What will you do? As far as anyone knows, you're not a believer. They still think that you're coming here to show me the error of my ways."

"Somebody does know I am a believer," replied Tom. "My wife. I told her after our last visit. You would not believe it, but she has been considering becoming a Christian for some years now. It's funny that we never talked about it. I would often notice that the Bible Jim had given me was moved from the place where I had left it. I thought Joan had just picked it up and moved it to clean. You know Jim's booklet. I had a copy that disappeared. It turns out that my wife took it and has read it over many times. She's been talking to Ellen Johansen. When I told her that I had given my life to Christ, she prayed and did the same. Is evangelism always that easy?"

"You had news like that and you came in with a long face! Glory be to God."

"She is afraid. She knows what her faith in Christ will mean. Now we have to tell our children."

"Yes, you must. Their minds have been turned away from Jesus in school and by the media. They may be the ones to turn you in. They've been instructed to do so, I understand. But by all means, you have to tell them. They need Jesus, too."

"Should we turn ourselves in as Christians on the fifteenth?" asked Tom sincerely.

"And steal away from the Supreme Leader the challenge of searching you out? You must never deny your faith in Christ, Tom, but that doesn't mean you have to turn yourself in. Tell others about your faith in Jesus but be careful when and to whom you witness.

You are in a position where you can help other believers. You must do that. You know that Jim is in the area again. Actually he has been for some time. He has met secretly several times with the believers in town. He's been hiding out with his family and in-laws at the Johansen house. Ellen looks in on them every few days, bringing them groceries and news. She won't be able to do it after the fifteenth. Her faith is too well known, and she herself will be in danger."

"How do you know all this?" asked Tom in amazement.

"If my fellow inmates can get drugs, I should certainly be able to get a little bit of information."

"What should I do?"

"How would you like to own a farm?"

"A farm," Tom laughed, "What do you mean?"

"The Simmons own a large farm outside of town. It's in an isolated area, nestled between several hills, and hidden from the main road. It would be a perfect place of refuge. The problem is that the Simmons have been very outspoken about their faith, and are sure to be some of the first ones arrested after the 16th. At this point, the farm is worthless to them and they are willing to sell it for a song. Consider this idea. If they sell it to you, and make it convincing that they are leaving, no one will suspect it as a hiding place for Christians. Your friends will think that you made a sly business deal, and will be jealous for not having been the ones to have fallen into it. For some time now, the believers of both Trinity Evangelical Lutheran Church and the Baptist Church have been preparing the farm. From what I understand, they are prepared to house semi-comfortably some 70 people and have stockpiled food for several months. Everything hinges, however, on the purchase of the farm by someone who is sympathetic to the Christian faith."

"And I could be that someone," Tom reflected thoughtfully.

"Exactly."

"Can it be done in time?"

"It has to be. We can't count on the Global Union to be as ambiguous about this issue as the United States has been."

"No, we can't," agreed Tom. "Commissioners from the Global Union come tomorrow night. With local help, they will be the new governing body of the town. I'm not sure where that will leave us, as the town council. A change in jobs might be good for me now. Do the Simmons know that you are proposing this to me?"

"No they don't," answered Peter, "but that won't be a problem. If you're willing to do it, go to them today and tell them that I sent you. Tell them that they are to sell the farm to you as soon as the papers can be readied for them to do so, and that they have to 'move' by early next week."

"I don't have much liquid cash, but I could get a mortgage on our house."

"The price isn't an issue, but getting a mortgage would help to camouflage things and give your purchase of the farm legitimacy," encouraged Peter. "But I think that you ought to remain as a member of the town council for as long as you can."

"I won't be able to, I'm sure, unless I'm willing to deny my faith in Jesus. They will demand that we swear allegiance to the Supreme Leader and the Global Union. It is better that I withdraw now, before I am asked to sign some document. I can base my protest on patriotism or something, and resign without much suspicion. And what of you my friend? I fear that this will be our last visit."

"It must be, though I shall miss you greatly," lamented Peter. "The one great cross I bear between now and my martyrdom, is having to listen to the endless propaganda piped into my cell. It's designed to convert me from my stubborn extremism. I would prefer the visits of Rev. Ebner to the mindless dribble they force me to listen to now. I understand that they will start depriving us of food next week and implement a bit of torture as part of their persuasion. I don't look forward to it, but I will soon be with my Lord. Rejoice with me. We will see one another in heaven."

"Yes, I trust we will. I thank God for the way he's used you in these visits that we've had together. I have to go, but before I do, I'd like to pray with you."

"And I with you my brother. O gracious and loving Heavenly Father," Peter began, without closing his eyes or changing his demeanor, "Thank you for your presence in this place. Thank you for Tom's visits," Peter's voice broke for the first time since Tom had known him, and tears came to his eyes. Although he did not like to show it, he had indeed been under a great deal of strain. "Thank you for Tom's visits," Peter continued, gaining control again over his emotions, "You know how much I needed them. Thank you for his courage in coming, for the sincerity of his searching heart, and for the genuine nature of his faith. Thank you, Lord, for this great news that his wife is also a believer, and we would ask you today for the souls of their three children. Oh God, give us courage for the coming days. May our lives give you pleasure. In the name of Jesus, I pray, amen."

Tom echoed the prayer of his friend with an "amen."

With that the two men rose, and Tom was about to embrace Peter, when they heard the knock on the door and saw the guard's face in the window. Stepping back away from Peter and opening the door, Tom added for the benefit of the guard, as well as his own, "And so you still stubbornly confess that we all are sinners and that faith in Jesus Christ alone can save, even knowing that to say so will soon mean your death."

"I do," replied Peter, smiling. "Praise God, I do."

"The prisoner is unrepentant," Tom said to the guard. "There is nothing more that I can do. He thinks you are the one who should repent!"

"Do think about it, Jerry," Peter said to the guard, as the door closed.

Chapter 18

The believers gathered around the television set at the Simmon/Watson farm. They were to be witnesses that day of the triumph of faith over the darkness and evil that had enshrouded them.

They turned off the sound on the television, until the names of the accused began to be read. They had no desire to hear the propaganda of the Global Union. Those dying for their faith were not given a microphone from which they might declare their last words. The Supreme Leader would not give them a forum for their rebellious heresies.

If the Supreme Leader could have seen them, he would have been very unhappy. The goal in broadcasting the executions was to scare people away from allegiance to a "God" and by so doing solidify their allegiance to himself and the Global Union. Instead, what it did, at least for the believers at the Watson farm, was to encourage them in their own faith and determination to serve Jesus until death.

The "show" took place in Madison, Wisconsin, the capital of the state. All of the "radical, extreme bigots" from throughout the state, had been brought together there for a mass execution. In spite of the frigid weather, thousands gathered outside of the State House to witness the executions. The killings, as with everything the Global Union did, were done in an efficient manner. Six guillotines were set up, one in between each of the white granite pillars of the State Capitol Building. The names of the accused were read off. One by one, the prisoners were led to the instrument that would cause their death. The crime, the same for each of the accused, was read off with each name, "treason against the State and the promotion of hatred and disunity among its citizens in the name of religious conviction." When an accused had been placed in each one of the six guillotines, the newly appointed Governor of the state dropped his arm and the guillotines did their deadly work in unison. The bodies of the dead were removed to a waiting truck, while the heads were placed in a second truck. It was evident that no respect would be afforded the bodies of these enemies of the state.

Former Governor Graham, wearing the same orange jump suit as the rest, was among the first group of six to be killed. Unbelievably, the crowd cheered as his head rolled into the bucket below. The believers gathered at the Watson farm wept.

Tears came to Jim's eyes, as he saw one pastor after another, men whom he had known and respected, meet their deaths that day in Madison. They were tears of sadness, but they were also tears of pride. In their silence, these men of God proclaimed eloquently their commitment to Jesus Christ as Lord. They were not broken or fearful. Their eyes shown brightly, and they offered no resistance to the captors. The majority of those being killed that day were evangelical pastors and leaders. Mixed among them were some Catholic priests and nuns, Jewish rabbis, Muslim clerics, and a few representatives of other lesser practiced faiths, all dying for what or for in whom they believed.

"Look," shouted Sandy, pointing to the television set. "Is that Jerry Leitzel?" Jerry Leitzel was the former pastor of the Presbyterian church in town, and nobody at the Watson Farm expected to see him being led to the guillotines.

"Well what do you know," exclaimed Sven Svensen, "it is him. Who would have expected to see Jerry up there? Didn't he take a pastorate in a church up in the north?"

"He sure did," said Jim, as surprised as everyone else. "It looks as if he changed more than his location. Glory be to God! I remember him commenting to me that the church had quite a strong 'born again' element in it, but that he was confident that he could tame them and redirect their enthusiasm towards tolerance, and ecumenical concerns and involvement. It looks as if he met Jesus along the way and had a change of plans. I guess he'll have opportunity to tell us about it when we meet together in glory."

After several more groups of six were martyred, the announcer read, "Peter Samuels, guilty, by his own testimony, of treason against the state and the promotion of hatred and disunity among its citizens in the name of religious conviction."

There was no noise in the living room. This was a sacred moment. All eyes where glued to the event occurring before them. Sandy wrapped her arms around Peter's wife, Judy. On their last visit together, Peter had agreed with her on a sign. As one last confession of commitment to Christ and one last profession of the Lord's goodness, even in the moment of his martyrdom, Peter would raise and lower his head three times and then would close his eyes. "In the name of the Father, the Son, and the Holy Spirit. Amen."

"Look, there it is," said Judy.

As the policeman led Peter to the guillotine where he would be killed, the camera focused in on him. He, like all the others had his hands cuffed behind him and his feet shackled, but his head was free. As he raised and lowed his head three times slowly, he spoke the words, and Judy spoke them with him. "In the name of the Father, the Son, and the Holy Spirit. Amen"

Then, with his eyes closed but his head raised, they could see him praying the words, "Father forgive them." He opened his eyes, and his demeanor was changed.

"Look," exclaimed George Simmons. "Look at his face."

They could look no longer, as Peter was pushed down into position by the police officer on his right, but they had all seen it, and they would talk much about it in the days ahead: "His eyes, they were fixed on something above, as if seeing someone in the heavens." "His face shone with a light that had nothing to do with the sun." "If a picture could be taken of the pure essence of peace and joy, it would have been Peter's face in that moment." "It was just like the story of Steven in the book of Acts. Peter was always a joyous person, but in a serious, formal sort of way... in that moment, his face was like a child's."

Had it really happened, or were they seeing what they hoped to see? Was the change in Peter's countenance, or had it been in their perception? They had not noticed anything similar in the faces of the individuals martyred prior to Peter, though each had died with dignity. What was certain and important was that they had seen it, and it served greatly to comfort and encourage them in that moment and in the days which followed.

After the weighted knife fell and did its bloody work, they turned off the television.

George Simmons read from Psalm 116:15 "Precious in the sight of the Lord is the death of his saints."

Sandy, still hugging Judy, quoted from Revelation 2:10, the passage which Peter had made famous among them: "Fear none of the things which you will suffer...Be faithful unto death, and I will give you a crown of life."

Sven quoted thoughtfully, "Let not your heart be troubled: You believe in God, believe also in me. In my Father's house are many mansions...I go to prepare a place for you. And if I go and prepare a place for you, I will come again, and receive you unto myself; that where I am you may be also."

"Blessed are you," Jim declared from Matthew 5, "when men shall revile you, and persecute you, and shall say all manner of evil against you falsely, for my sake. Rejoice, and be exceedingly glad: for great is your reward in heaven: for so persecuted they the prophets which were before you."

Joan, the newest of the believers there, said, with the apostle Paul, "For me to live is Christ, and to die is gain."

Mr. Peterson caressed the words of Paul in 1 Corinthians 13:12, "For now we see through a glass, darkly; but then face to face."

Judy, through tears of sadness and at the same time joy, put their situation in perspective. Fumbling with her Bible a moment, she finally found the passage she was looking for. In trembling voice, intermixed with pauses and sobs, she began, "My dear friends. I want you to know where my dearest Peter is right now. It is also important that we know what is ahead of us. I read from Revelation 6:9-11, 'And when he had opened the fifth seal, I saw under the altar the souls of them that were slain for the word of God, and for the testimony which they held: And they cried with a loud voice, saying. How long, O Lord, holy and true, do you not judge and avenge our blood on them that dwell on the earth? And white robes were given unto every one of them; and it was said unto them, that they should rest yet for a little season, until their fellow servants also and their brethren, that should be killed as they were, should be fulfilled.'

* * * *

If you would like to write us, we would like to hear from you. Our address is: Paul and Sherri Nilsen, Camino de Bugeo, #1, 29180 Riogordo SPAIN.

Printed in the United States
18805LVS00001B/67-117